TRAPPED IN
DECEPTION

Ken Webb

ISBN 979-8-9932667-0-1

Copyright © 2024 by **Ken Webb**
Registered with the U.S. Copyright Office
Registration Number TXu 2-417-687

Formatter **@lunyzln** (Instagram)
Cover art by **Bilal Haider**
Webbinator Publishing

DEDICATION

I dedicate this book, first and foremost, to my grandmother, Ethel Leibfreid, who believed in me when others did not. When my elementary school labeled me "mildly retarded" and said I would never learn to read, she refused to accept that. She devoted her spare time to teach me—patiently and lovingly—until the words came alive. After one summer with her, I returned to school reading two grade levels ahead. Her belief in me changed the course of my life and instilled in me a love for reading and writing that continues to this day.

This book was written during one of the most painful chapters I've ever experienced. My best friend, Cecilia, died while I was living in Peru. I was by her side. Just three months later, my mother passed away, and I was with her in Texas. Two months after that, her brother—my uncle—died in Pennsylvania, and I was there as well. Grief surrounded me, but so did love. My cousins stood by me during that time, giving me strength when mine was fading.

I am also grateful to the *All About Writing* group on Facebook, whose thoughtful insights and steady encouragement kept me moving forward. To the passionate language teachers at *El Sol* in Miraflores, Lima—thank you for inspiring so much of what this book became. My years in the Army, my work with the Department of Defense, and my time with American

Airlines have shaped how I see the world, and my travels continue to teach and stretch me in ways I never expected.

To my friends—your encouragement has meant more than words can express. Your belief in me, especially when I falter, continues to lift me and keep me moving forward as I pursue the next chapters of my dreams.

"The worst lies
are the lies we tell
ourselves."

Richard Bach

CHARACTER GUIDE

Main Characters

Eddy Ludt
- Age: 45 (turns 46 during the novel).
- Appearance: 6'2", average build, weathered face with sharp features; his brownish hazel eyes convey intensity and guardedness.
- Profession: Lieutenant Colonel, U.S. Army Reserves; employee at Ultimate Flights (resigns during the novel).
- Background: Eddy is a disciplined Army reservist who feels disillusioned with civilian life. He works in IT at an airline until he resigns to take on a dangerous mission. Burdened with internal doubts and haunted by past decisions, he searches for renewed purpose through action.
- Personality: Intelligent, introspective, highly strategic, but reserved and self-conscious. He has a dry wit, a deeply ingrained sense of duty, and values loyalty over ambition. He is a methodical thinker, an analyst, but not a quick thinker, and he's challenged when called upon to do so.

Shawn Michael Larson (alias Michael Buster and Shawn McFadden)
- Age: 47.
- Appearance: 6'3", athletic build with broad shoulders and big hands, sharp features, piercing blue eyes. He is exceptionally handsome.

- Profession: Financial analyst/CFO of Trufunds. He is an expert con artist.
- Background: Fakes his own death after stealing a large sum of money. Flees to Peru to plan yet another great heist (he never has enough). Manipulates people and systems for personal gain.
- Personality: Cold, predatory, calculating, and seductive. Skilled at deception and willing to exploit anyone. No empathy, no remorse, only results.

Military & Tactical Personnel

Donald Delcey
- Age: 42.
- Appearance: Solid build, commanding yet calm presence. Wiry muscles.
- Profession: Special Forces soldier and schoolteacher.
- Background: Serves as Eddy's confidant during mission preparation. He does not participate in the mission, but he is a trusted go-between of Peter Zhao, Wise Dog, and Eddy. His demeanor is stable and dependable.
- Personality: Levelheaded, supportive, wise both in and out of combat.

Wise Dog
- Age: 44.
- Appearance: Muscular, tattooed, disciplined posture.
- Profession: Former Special Forces operative and currently a mercenary working for Silent Wolf.
- Background: Tactical expert brought in to train and assist with operations.
- Personality: Quiet, methodical, intense. His silence and presence demand respect.

Peter Zhao
- Age: 39.
- Appearance: Slender and quick-footed. Quietly confident.
- Profession: Silent Wolf employee who also does mercenary work on the side. Involved with Silent Wolf through family ties.
- Background: Nephew of Tommy Chong. Supports operations indirectly and observes with tactical awareness.
- Personality: Respectful, intelligent, reliable. A womanizer.

Staff Sergeant Mark O'Hagan
- Age: 57 (in the flashback scene).
- Appearance: A heavyset, imposing build with a gruff exterior.
- Profession: Veteran Non-Commissioned Officer of both the Marine Corps and the United States Army. In civilian life, he is a police officer with the Fort Worth Police Department.
- Background: Close personal friend of Eddy Ludt. Nearing retirement. A respected, battle-tested mentor who shares a bond with Eddy built on years of trust.
- Personality: Blunt, loyal, practical, and honorable. A quiet protector who commands respect.

Sergeant First Class Doreman.
- Age: 38 (in the flashback scene).
- Appearance: Very tall (6'6"), extremely thin, always alert.
- Profession: Senior NCO.

- Background: Skeptical of Eddy's readiness during early deployment phases, but executes his role with precision.
- Personality: Calculating, vigilant, professional.

Sergeant Charley Hadderton.
- Age: 26 (in the flashback scene).
- Appearance: Short, slightly overweight, youthful.
- Profession: Army Reserve Soldier.
- Background: Green and overeager, but genuinely wants to prove himself.
- Personality: Loyal, naïve, sometimes unintentionally humorous.

Captain Douglas.
- Age: 34 (in the flashback scene).
- Appearance: Athletic, confident, clean-cut.
- Profession: U.S. Army Officer.
- Background: Eddy's commanding officer. Calm and respected in high-stress situations.
- Personality: Rational, competent, leadership oriented.

Bismillah Khan Mohammadi.
- Age: 43 (in the flashback scene).
- Appearance: bearded, strong, commanding presence.
- Profession: Afghan interpreter and cultural advisor.
- Background: Trusted liaison during Eddy's deployment.
- Personality: Reserved, dignified, clear-headed in conflict zones.

Trufunds Bank & Financial Characters

Carlos Ortiz.
- Age: 60.
- Appearance: Short (5'5"), overweight, graying hair, glasses.
- Profession: CEO of Trufunds Bank.
- Background: Military veteran and now a corporate powerhouse with a bloated ego and a deteriorating moral compass.
- Personality: Self-serving, manipulative, increasingly paranoid.

Tommy Chong.
- Age: 60.
- Appearance: Asian American, sturdy frame, upright posture.
- Profession: Head of Security at Trufunds.
- Background: Military veteran and uncle to Peter Zhao. Loyal to Carlos. Former detective with the Dallas Police Force.
- Personality: Cautious, old-school, values personal friendships.

Diane Ferry.
- Age: 25.
- Appearance: Blond, attractive, sun-kissed complexion. Dresses professionally but with flair.
- Profession: Personal Assistant to Carlos.
- Background: Easily flattered by attention. Her ambition and flirtations make her a perfect target for Shawn's manipulation. Recent transplant to Dallas, Texas. Originally from Collingdale, Pennsylvania.

- Personality: Flirtatious, image-conscious, detached from consequences.

Lemont Finley.
- Age: 28.
- Appearance: 5'5", overweight, greasy hair, thick glasses, unkempt.
- Profession: Programmer.
- Background: Writes code for Shawn without understanding the criminal implications, but suspects something shady is going on.
- Personality: Smart but naïve. Socially awkward and desperate for validation. A loner with few friends.

William.
- Age: 58.
- Appearance: Tall, thinning hair, weary.
- Profession: Longtime Trufunds employee.
- Personality: Cynical, disengaged, and jaded.

Brian.
- Age: 39.
- Appearance: Blond, wiry, visibly nervous.
- Profession: Trufunds employee.
- Personality: Anxious, high-strung, observant.

Rebecca.
- Age: 28.
- Appearance: Dark-haired, attractive, Colombian.
- Profession: Works at Trufunds.
- Personality: Friendly, open, courteous.

Jason.
- Age: 23.

- Appearance: Slender, glasses, prematurely balding.
- Profession: Intern at Trufunds.
- Personality: Eager, awkward, deferential.

Mercenaries & Illegal Operations

Frederico Ramirez.
- Age: 36.
- Appearance: Muscular, heavily tattooed, intimidating.
- Profession: Former 7th Special Forces Group member. Mercenary/security.
- Background: Enforcer hired by Shawn.
- Personality: Physically dominant, enjoys control, confrontational.

Manuel Flores.
- Age: 35.
- Appearance: Short, muscular, intense gaze.
- Profession: Former 7th Special Forces Group member. Mercenary/security.
- Background: Works with Frederico; loyal and dangerous.
- Personality: Obedient, volatile, direct.

Civilians, Travelers & Support Characters

Johnny Croenen.
- Age: 40.
- Appearance: Rugged, scruffy, weathered from combat and hard living.
- Profession: Pilot and former Army sniper.
- Background: Freelance smuggler and transport operator.

- Personality: Bold, cocky, unpredictable.

Miriami Morales.
- Age: 34.
- Appearance: Sharp, composed.
- Profession: Co-pilot.
- Background: Johnny's fiancée; stays quiet but observes everything.
- Personality: Calm, low-profile, competent.

Anna Maria Haywood.
- Age: 37.
- Appearance: Redhead, casual dress, slightly worn from stress.
- Profession: None, recently divorced.
- Background: Unwitting pawn in Shawn's plan; her credit cards and presence are exploited.
- Personality: Kind, trusting, emotionally fragile.

Pedro Leandro.
- Age: 38.
- Appearance: Clean-cut, ponytail, nervous but educated.
- Profession: Spanish teacher.
- Background: Hired to teach Eddy Spanish. Feels out of place around weapons. Highly educated.
- Personality: Respectful, professional, adaptable.

Gustavo.
- Age: 42.
- Appearance: Slender, clean appearance.
- Profession: Front desk clerk, Marriott.
- Background: Reluctantly manipulated by Shawn.
- Personality: Helpful, hesitant, easily pressured.

Harold Stivey.
- Age: 52.
- Appearance: Military-cut hair, sharp demeanor.
- Profession: Security consultant.
- Background: Former military intelligence. Immediately suspicious of Shawn.
- Personality: Analytical, skeptical, principled.

Claudia.
- Age: 14.
- Appearance: Young, responsible neighborhood girl.
- Profession: Student.
- Background: Lives two doors down from Eddy; takes care of Dina.
- Personality: Trustworthy, kind, dependable.

Huancayo Characters

Father Benavides.
- Age: 62.
- Appearance: Modest attire, intense eyes, clean appearance.
- Profession: Catholic priest.
- Background: Stands up to Shawn, protects a young boy from exploitation, and refuses a bribe.
- Personality: Brave, incorruptible, unwavering in faith and ethics.

Sam Baker.
- Age: 41.
- Appearance: Worn jeans, scruffy face, slightly sunburned.
- Profession: Ex-Silicon Valley techie.

- Background: Burned out, smokes weed, supports Shawn with surveillance.
- Personality: Detached, philosophical, burned out but tech-savvy.

Airline Staff

Nelly.
- Age: 30.
- Appearance: Friendly, attractive, confident.
- Profession: Delta Airlines ticket agent.
- Background: Helps Shawn and Anna Maria during check-in.
- Personality: Personable, upbeat, charmed easily.

Anita.
- Age: 45.
- Appearance: Professional demeanor.
- Profession: American Airlines counter agent.
- Background: Helps Eddy process firearm paperwork.
- Personality: Calm, no-nonsense.

🐾 Animal

Dina (the Dog).
- Age: 4.
- Appearance: German Shepherd/Collie mix. Medium-sized, alert, attentive.
- Profession: Companion dog.
- Background: Cared for by Eddy's Mom while Eddy is deployed.
- Personality: Loyal, affectionate, intelligent.

Table of Contents

CHAPTER 1:
DEFINING SHAWN
MICHAEL LARSON

Monday, 22 December 2014, 0800 hours
Trufunds headquarters, Dallas, Texas

Shawn Larson never wasted an opportunity to take what wasn't his. On this morning, while Dallas was wrapped in festive cheer, Shawn was executing the most dangerous con of his career.

Meticulously planned, it all began ten years ago when he'd assumed a new identity, Michael Buster, and maneuvered his way into a job at Trufunds, Texas' most successful bank. A decade later, he was CFO. His résumé was pure fiction: a Wharton graduate, certified project manager, and expert in corporate ethics. However, no one at Trufunds had ever heard of him before he arrived.

That was by design.

While the office hummed with Christmas carols, Shawn sat in his office, untouched by the holiday spirit. At six-foot-three, his self-assured smile and perfect white teeth were reassuring. Dark blond hair. Chiseled jaw. The picture of success. Shawn always smiled in a way that put people at ease. He was precisely the kind of man others admired. But inside, Shawn was a predator.

They gave me everything. A smirk curled at the corner of his mouth as he finalized the last piece of paperwork.

The holiday season meant a reprieve for most of the Trufunds employees. For Shawn, work was just beginning. The walls were closing in, but the millions soon to hit an offshore account would secure his future. It would be the last step before his disappearance—unless someone unexpected got in the way.

But Shawn had accounted for every variable. Or so he believed.

In the breakroom, Brian and William were swapping office gossip. The air smelled of stale coffee.

William, in his late fifties, sat hunched, dark plastic glasses perched on his nose. His six-foot-one frame had a slight stoop, and his thinning hair betrayed the toll the years had taken on him. Brian, younger at thirty-nine, was wiry and jittery, his blond hair receding, worn down by the strain of working in Shawn's shadow. He took another sip of the bitter coffee, his eyes tired and bloodshot.

"I prepared all of Mr. Buster's spreadsheets," Brian muttered under his breath, annoyed. *A little recognition, just once...* His frustration was starting to boil over.

William smirked, setting his mug down. "Careful with that, overtime, Brian. Trufunds doesn't exactly reward it."

Brian rolled his eyes. "Mr. Buster told me not to log it. Said he'd make it up to me with a bonus at the end of the year." He snorted.

The door swung open, and in walked Michael Buster himself. He scanned the room like he owned the place and honed in on the coffee pot. To the other men in the room, his presence cut like a cold breeze.

"Hey, bros, what's happening?" Shawn grinned, his smile wide and full of self-assurance.

William and Brian instantly straightened, stiff with forced politeness. Shawn didn't even notice. He walked past them, grabbing a plate of holiday treats left on the counter without asking whose they were.

The room felt like his stage, and everyone else was just extras in the play of his life. He poured himself the last of the coffee and left the empty pot on the counter.

Then the door opened again. A man in his mid-fifties, leaning on a crutch, stepped in. When he saw Shawn, he froze, and after a beat, limped out again quickly, the speed of his exit surprising for someone in his condition.

Brian wondered why this man was acting strangely. "Who is that?"

William raised an eyebrow. "That was Mark. Broke his leg last year in some accident."

Shawn chewed slowly, the cookie in his mouth barely registering. "Interesting," he muttered, more to the air than to anyone. His smile faltered for half a second. Then it was back, smooth and impenetrable.

3

He left without another word.

Brian and William sat in silence for a moment, the weight of Buster's indifference—Shawn's indifference—pressing down on them.

"He's not gonna give me that bonus, is he, Will?" Brian asked, his voice resigned, the edge of bitterness clear.

William stared into his cup before answering. "Not a chance, buddy. Try not to let it get to you."

"You ever notice how he never listens to anyone?"

"Oh, he listens," William said. "Just not to us. We don't matter."

Brian frowned, shaking his head. "How the hell did he move up through the ranks so fast? What's his secret?"

William leaned in, his voice dropping to a near whisper. "He does exactly what he did to us. He plays the game—charms the people above him, seduces them, and then conquers them. Then when they're no longer useful, he tosses them aside like used tissues."

On his way to his office, Shawn stopped at the restroom in the hall and didn't bother flushing. *Not my problem,* he thought, a smile tugging at his lips. He felt untouchable.

As he passed coworkers in the hall, he gave them the barest of nods, his eyes fixed on his goal. *They have no idea.* He closed his office door behind him and hung his jacket neatly on the hook.

Even his marriage had been a transaction. He'd married Alicia for her wealth, discarded her when she was no longer useful, and walked away richer. Her tearful voicemails were nothing more than an echo in his mind, quickly forgotten. She cried the night he'd walked out. He never even slowed down.

He didn't need companionship. He didn't need love. This con would be the last thing he ever needed.

As he signed some documents, a rare flicker of doubt surfaced. *What if someone notices? What if they put it together?*

It was a brief intrusion, something he never allowed himself to entertain. Shawn shook it off, replacing the doubt with certainty.

It doesn't matter. No one can touch me. Not now, not ever.

The algorithm was beautiful: it bypassed firewalls, extracted funds from dormant accounts, and rerouted the money to offshore havens. Small amounts, unnoticeable. Fifty bucks from a million? No one noticed. The same amount from a thousand-dollar account? Too risky.

As the final transfer was executed, "100% COMPLETE" flashed across the screen. Shawn wiped the drive, even his browsing history. There was no evidence to be found without a forensic sweep of the computer.

The last piece was the private drive of Carlos Ortiz, the CEO of Trufunds. Shawn cracked the encryption and downloaded the data to the 4TB hard drive. This key would earn Shawn an additional five million in cryptocurrency linked to illegal gambling. Even if the bank discovered it, they wouldn't report it. No one wanted law enforcement digging into that mess. *Who's the bigger crook? I'm just better at it.*

A twisted grin curled his lips. He divided the funds among accounts in the Bahamas, the Cayman Islands, and Europe. It was done.

For a moment, Shawn felt a tingling sensation in his spine. Had it been too easy? "Perfect plans" had ways of hiding their flaws. He pushed the thought away with a scoff. Fear, he reminded himself, was a weakness he'd outgrown long ago, a waste of his precious time.

Shawn pulled a small notebook from his pocket and leafed through it until he found the number he was looking for. He pulled his cell phone out of his pocket, unlocked it, and dialed the number listed in the notebook.

It rang once.

"Maggio's Pizza?" a voice answered.

"Hi, can I get a double pepperoni delivered to the Trufunds lobby? Name's Henry Sanchen," Shawn said.

He ended the call. The code phrase was sent. Shawn's contacts would know what it meant.

He texted a few final confirmations, then smashed the SIM card and flushed the remains in his office toilet. Every move was covered.

Satisfied, he played the plan over again in his mind, checking for cracks. There were none. Not this time.

He had a chip on his shoulder he'd never admit. But it was there, fueling him, haunting him. If people had given him credit for his brilliance, maybe he wouldn't have done this. Then again, even Shawn knew he would have done it regardless. Even he believed his lies most of the time. In his heart, using people was part of him. It always had been.

Shawn left his office and rode the private elevator to the lobby. When he stepped outside into the cold December air, he moved like he owned the world.

"One more game to win," he muttered, almost smiling. "Then I disappear."

CHAPTER 2:
GET YOUR GOLDEN GOOSE WELL-FED AND DRESSED BEFORE YOU KILL IT.

Friday, 19 December 2014, 1800 hours
The Experience restaurant, downtown Dallas, Texas

Some problems can't be solved, only erased. Lemont was one of them.

Shawn couldn't risk a backend savant unraveling everything with a few keystrokes. A simple kill-and-dump would trigger a search. Lemont needed to be found dead, not murdered.

He took the unsuspecting lamb out to a steak and lobster dinner at The Experience in downtown Dallas. The rich aroma of cigars mingled with the slightly intoxicating fragrance of aged wood and leather. At the bar, Shawn ordered soda water with lime and told the bartender to call it a gin and tonic.

Lemont, a man unbound by social norms and conventions, was treated like royalty, the beer flowing freely while Shawn sipped his mocktail. He let the lime-scented soda roll over his tongue, wishing it burned. Spending any amount of time with Lemont was about as enjoyable as a colonoscopy, as he had the emotional intelligence of a coffee table.

The geek was a pudgy, awkward man in his late twenties. His round face was perpetually flushed as if he'd just walked up a flight of stairs. A pair of thick, smudged glasses rested on his bulbous nose, slightly crooked from an old accident. That, along with thinning, greasy brown hair that clung to his scalp, gave him a disheveled appearance.

His personal hygiene was hit-or-miss; Lemont showered enough to be passable but often forgot details like deodorant or brushing his hair. His hunched posture and fidgeting hands betrayed an underlying nervous energy, especially when talking to women, who rarely gave him a second glance.

His voice carried a nasal whine, and he often trailed off mid-sentence, like when he said, *"Well, I guess if you wanted to, um... never mind."*

The evening ground on like a dentist's drill. Shawn forced a smile through Lemont's obscure anecdotes and glanced at his watch when the geek wasn't looking.

Lemont said, "Gosh, Mike, I don't ever have to work for those assholes again if I don't want to."

The only person Shawn knew who was better with a computer than Lemont was Eddy Ludt, a former friend.

Shawn flattered Lemont. "With your skills, I would think you'd want to start your own company and give Jobs and Gates a run for their money." *I wonder when this loser last had a date. Probably never been laid.* "Don't forget us little people when you make it big. Remember your friend Michael, who helped finance your dream and enabled you to achieve escape velocity."

"Do you really think I could be that big, Mike?" Lemont gasped. "I always wanted to be rich and famous."

"Sure, man, you could go to comic-cons every week." Shawn paused. "Say, I bet you'll pick up a lot of girls in that shiny new Corvette I gave you." *Never mind, they'll think you're a creep with mommy issues.* "Let me guess, you go for the mind?"

"As long as those minds come in nice packages," Lemont shot back with a teenage-girl giggle.

Lemont, slightly unsteady from the alcohol, seemed oblivious to the dangers that lurked behind his companion's pleasant smile and calm voice. He was more engrossed in his phone, scanning social media and living in an imaginary world. It was a gesture that might seem rude to anyone else, but Shawn didn't mind. It helped.

"Are you sure you don't want to be friends on Facebook? We can stay in touch and hang out," Lemont offered.

I would rather bathe in raw cow meat and be slowly eaten alive by piranhas.

You won't be talking to anyone tomorrow. "Maybe, if I can figure it out. How about I call you tomorrow and you talk me through it?"

Shawn feigned ignorance about social media. He had some accounts under different names, he used to track people, but he never used his own photo. Since

11

almost everyone used social media, it was a useful source for collecting information, especially for malicious purposes or blackmail. Still, he never wanted anyone to do the same to him. Even his email accounts changed after every significant job.

As another round of drinks arrived, Shawn leaned in with predatory anticipation. "So, Lemont, I'm absolutely fascinated by this algorithm you've created. How does it work?"

Shawn narrowed his eyes as the man launched into a long-winded explanation. *My God, I bet this is the highlight of your week. You're not just a nerd—you're a black belt in irrelevance. How can someone be so intelligent and so utterly stupid at the same time?*

Shawn understood the fundamentals of the algorithm, but real control meant finding the hidden backdoor. He needed to modify its purpose and function seamlessly, ensuring it remained undetected until long after he'd faded into an unfortunate statistic. Achieving this level of control meant uncovering more of the algorithm's hidden capabilities—knowledge only Lemont could provide.

Lemont was already on his second beer by the time he finished explaining.

The server whisked away the appetizer plates. The thick smell of butter and grilled meat lingered in the air. *This guy is easy.*

Shawn reclined slightly, measuring him. "So... tell me, Lemont. Be honest. How long did it take you to build this thing?"

Lemont grinned, and his cheeks were flushed. "Longer than you'd think. The math was brutal. But once the core logic clicked, man... it practically wrote itself."

Shawn laughed. *He's getting really intoxicated. Good.* "I've seen it run. It's beautiful. Clean. Elegant. Hell, I almost want to frame it." He lowered his voice. "I did notice something weird, though. Tried to poke around the edges, maybe tweak a thing or two, but I got locked out. Kicked me straight to the desktop like I broke it."

"That's by design, my friend," Lemont smirked, tapping his temple. "You didn't pay me to build a sandbox. You paid me to build a vault."

Shawn laughed lightly. "Right, right. Just didn't expect it to be that airtight." He paused, giving Lemont a long look. "But let's say I need to adjust it later—real-world changes. Priorities shift. I mean, there's gotta be a backdoor, right?"

Lemont chuckled. "Oh, there's a back door. But it only opens for me."

Shawn tilted his head. "Meaning what?"

"Meaning if you want to make changes, you need the override code."

"A code?" Shawn raised his eyebrows. "One word? Phrase? What are we talking about?"

Lemont grinned again, clearly enjoying the moment. "Just one line. Built straight into the validation routine. Without it, you're dead in the water. But don't worry. Nothing shady. You got what you paid for."

"Of course. ... for peace of mind in case I want to expand the system later, what's the code?"

Lemont hesitated. The alcohol had him relaxed, but there was a sliver of caution in his eyes. "I usually don't give that out."

Shawn leaned in with an endearing smile and full eye contact. "Lemont, come on. I just gave you more gold than Fort Knox and a Corvette with your name on it. Help me sleep better at night."

Lemont studied him for a moment, then shrugged. "Alright. Just don't go screwing it up." He picked up a cocktail napkin and a pen from the table. Slowly, carefully, he wrote:

lemont_1411

He slid the napkin across the table like it was a poker chip.

Shawn stared at it just long enough to burn it into memory. He folded it and slipped it into his pocket with a nod.

That's all I need. The algorithm was brilliant, but brilliance alone couldn't beat security. Banks had layers of redundancy, anomaly detection, and auditors trained to smell blood in the water.

But Shawn handled that months ago. He'd manipulated internal logs, corrupted protocols, and exploited overlooked legacy systems. When suspicion finally surfaced, it would be too late. The trail would vanish. Or better yet, point elsewhere. It wasn't just about beating the system. It was about deceiving the people who believed in it.

Lemont started to sway, his eyes glassy. Spit glistened at the corner of his mouth. The alcohol was beginning to clog his bloodstream, slowing everything down.

Shawn sat expressionless, calculating the next step. Earlier, he'd traded a stolen Honda Accord for a vial of uncut cocaine. He had stashed it in his coat pocket before dinner. When Lemont went to the restroom, Shawn scanned the restaurant. No one was watching. He unwrapped a napkin, crushed two digoxin tablets into powder, tapped in a bump of cocaine, and stirred it into Lemont's drink. He'd decided the frog-in-boiling-water approach would work best. Gradual, invisible. Lemont would go easy.

By midnight, the bar had mainly emptied, and Lemont was slurring his words, blinking slowly, and leaning too far forward. He was going in stages, his drink nearly gone. His mind was fading. His fate was sealed.

If the body were found quickly, the tox screen would say he'd made bad decisions. If not, no one would bother checking. That's why Shawn chose this restaurant, new to them both. No familiarity. No questions. Everything is paid in cash. He would never talk. Not online. Not to the cops. Not to anyone.

They left together, Lemont reeking of liquor and fast food. Shawn walked beside him, steadily as a blade.

"Hey, bro, you've really been putting it away tonight. Let me be your chauffeur," Shawn offered, nodding toward the new Corvette.

Lemont laughed and swayed. "Thanks, Mike. You think your Honda's safe here?"

Shawn didn't smile. "Yeah. We're friends. I take care of my friends. The Bible says we're our brother's keeper. Do unto others, right? Your safety means more to me than one of my cars."

"Yeah, I had a blast, man. You're a real one."

"Good. Let's get you home." Shawn opened the passenger door. "You need water or anything?" *You should be grateful I'm even letting you breathe the same air as me. Guys like you carry my bags and hope I tip well.*

"Nah. I'm good."

Shawn helped him in, and Lemont's head knocked against the frame. Shawn chuckled. *This idiot couldn't tell bleach from vodka right now.*

He pulled out of the lot with deliberate calm, not wanting to draw attention to the bright-red sports car.

At Lemont's complex, Shawn parked and studied the mess beside him. Lemont's shirt was soaked with sweat. A line of drool hung from his lip.

"Duuude," Lemont slurred, "you sure you don't wanna smoke with me? I got this Purple Kush from a Jamaican guy. Good stuff."

No friends. No self-respect. Just a rotting animal trying to stay conscious.

"I don't touch drugs. My church doesn't allow it. Body's a temple, brother," Shawn said gently. "Besides, I think you've had enough for one night."

Or enough for the rest of your life.

Lemont collapsed against the door while trying to stand, and Shawn caught his arm, helping him to his feet. Lemont stumbled forward, thick legs struggling to obey. Shawn let him lean against him, hot breath and sweat clinging to his skin.

Every movement served a purpose. Shawn's arms supported him with practiced ease, muscles built in the gym for moments like this. Lemont had the coordination of a kicked trash can.

They reached the door after five long minutes filled with burps, stumbles, and one last indignity. Lemont had pissed himself.

Great. Burning these clothes.

"Thanks for being my friend, Mike," Lemont muttered.

Shawn gave him a soft smile. "Glad you had fun."

If you puke on me, I'm putting you down early.

Lemont fumbled with his keys. Shawn took over, unlocked the door, and guided him inside.

No alarm. No code. Just trust in a zip code. Perfect.

He led him upstairs. At the bedroom door, Shawn gave him a gentle push, and Lemont collapsed face-first onto the bed, shoes still on.

Shawn turned, went downstairs, grabbed his backpack from the Corvette, and walked three blocks.

Raising his arm, he hailed a cab to the topless bar where he'd parked a black 2010 Camry. He got in the Camry and drove to a gas station, bought water, and changed in the restroom. Blue sweatpants, white sneakers, a black jacket, and a cap. He dumped his old clothes in the trash out back before driving back to the condo.

Armed with latex gloves, Shawn retrieved a bag of drugs from his trunk—weed, pills, a little coke—and spread them around Lemont's living room. He wiped down every surface he remembered touching during the earlier visit.

The condo was absurd. State-of-the-art electronics. Stacks of comics. A lineup of action figures on every shelf. *A grown man playing house with plastic heroes.*

He checked his watch. Time.

The drug concoction Shawn had slipped into Lemont's drink wasn't designed to kill immediately. It scrambled the heart's electrical signals, let chaos bloom in silence until it was too late. The alcohol numbed Lemont's awareness as the cocaine masked the warning signs. His breathing would slow. Pulse would stagger. But Shawn needed confirmation.

He needed Lemont dead before questions were asked, or his sliver of a conscience finally woke up.

He walked down the hall, eyes passing over posters of superheroes. Spider-Man. Iron Man. Captain America. *Men in costumes. Symbols for boys who never grew up.*

He entered the bedroom. Lemont was still sprawled on the bed, face down. Shawn stood over him.

Lemont stirred, hand twitching. His eyes fluttered.

As Shawn watched, Lemont flinched and jerked, then stiffened. Eyes rolled back. Breath hitched. Then nothing.

Shawn felt nothing. He usually didn't. That was the gift.

He waited, watched.

No twitch. No breath. Not even a sound. It was done.

He stepped back.

The autopsy would conclude alcohol, cocaine, and an obese heart past its limit. No one would test for digoxin unless they had a reason. And nobody did.

He'd watched the light fade from Lemont's eyes not out of malice but curiosity, like observing the last flicker in a dying filament. One of Lemont's eyes had remained half-lidded as if in mid-thought. *Put me out of my misery—that's what his body was saying. Message received.*

Shawn walked downstairs. No rush. He reviewed every motion. He dropped Lemont's keys on the floor near the front door to make it look as though Lemont had stumbled inside, drunk and high.

Everything Lemont told him had checked out. Real name. Real job. Real access. Real fool. *A man like that doesn't lie about things that matter.*

A perfect candidate for the Darwin Award.

Shawn smiled.

He retrieved the gold from the Corvette and placed it in a suitcase in the Camry's trunk. Then he got in, lit a cigarette, took a sip from the flask in his jacket, and pressed play on the CD player. Chopin drifted softly through the car.

Shawn drove with care, every turn measured, each mile wiping the night's work from his trail.

Murder didn't bother him. Consequences did. Lemont was a smear on the pavement of society. But the law would still call it murder. By morning, Lemont would be just another body.

And Shawn? Already gone.

CHAPTER 3:
PRIDE COMES BEFORE THE FALL

Monday, 22 December 2014, 1600 hours
Shawn's office at Trufunds headquarters, Dallas, Texas

Shawn leaned back in his leather chair at Trufunds Bank, a rare smile pulling at his mouth like a tic. The algorithm was a success! His ill-gotten fortune was now scattered across offshore accounts and embedded within a cryptocurrency key stored on an external hard drive. Untouchable. Untraceable—thanks to the work of one sad loner.

Shawn's future looked bright, but he wasn't yet in the clear.

He knew Trufunds ran offshore scams and laundered cartel money. They had ties to men who solved problems with a gun, not a lawyer. Eventually, someone would find Lemont dead when he didn't show up for work or pay his bills, but Shawn had plenty of time.

It was Monday. Shawn stared at the clock: four twenty in the afternoon. The fatigue hit him like a wave. He needed a caffeine hit.

He pressed the buzzer on his desk. "Diane, can you bring me coffee and some biscuits?"

Shawn's indulgence didn't stop at cigars or whiskey. It included Diane Ferry.

She was twenty-five, blond, and hungry. Diane had a magnetic charm. Her light hair flowed to her shoulders, blue eyes sparking with mischief, and her lips wore her favorite red lipstick like armor.

She was from Collingdale, Pennsylvania. She used to take the trolley to 69th Street in South Philadelphia, wearing jeans that had seen better days, to look for good deals on clothes. Diane was married to a corporate attorney thirty years her senior, but Michael was exciting. *He cares about me, right?* Wrong. Completely wrong, you idiot. She didn't think about the long term. She climbed and flirted. She collected every text, voicemail, and email that could be used later, a private insurance policy.

Carlos Ortiz, the CEO of Trufunds, had once been her target. But he discarded her, annoyed by her constant need for attention. Michael was more useful. He treated her like a person, not an accessory.

Diane had been Ortiz's assistant—and his plaything. She knew the codes to every door Shawn needed. Ortiz never changed them. Shawn asked to use those codes to access places he wasn't authorized to visit. He always said the same thing: "Sometimes you have to do what's best for the company, even if it's against the rules."

Diane entered with the coffee—kopi luwak. She smiled and placed it on his desk, porcelain cup and all.

Shawn inhaled the scent of her perfume. Her lipstick shimmered under the lights. Kopi luwak came from beans excreted by civets, little jungle cats. The finest gourmet feces on the planet. *Bon appétit.*

"Everything OK, Mike?" she asked.

"Fine," he said. "Just a lot to do. I'll finish tomorrow."

"Need anything else?"

He shook his head. "Take the rest of the day off. Count it as a Christmas gift."

She grinned. "Thanks, Mike."

He slapped her backside as she turned. She giggled and left.

Crossing the room, his shoes sank into thick blue carpet that smelled like a new car. The coffee burned his throat a little when he sipped it.

He picked up the cigar cutter and lighter, both engraved "S.L." Sam Leonard, he would say. A dear friend. Died in Iraq—gift from the family. Tears always came on cue. But Harold Stivey never bought it.

Harold, a reservist with an MP battalion under I MEF during Operation Enduring Freedom, had an eye for bullshit. He asked questions. Too many. Shawn dodged everyone.

Shawn never served. Claimed asthma. But he told the story with regret.

He smoked, drank, and went over the plan again, making sure there were no cracks. No variables. Just execution.

His phone buzzed—unknown number.

He stared.
Then it buzzed again.

CHAPTER 4:
THE GRAND EXIT

Monday, 22 December 2014, 1730 hours
Shawn's office at Trufunds headquarters, Dallas, Texas

He'd planned this escape three years in advance. Thursday was the break in the Trufunds' armor. Everyone would be gone long enough for him to disappear.

Trufunds shut down whenever a holiday landed on a Thursday. That gave Shawn four full days to vanish unnoticed until at least the following Monday. *Heck, with this skeleton crew, I probably have until after New Year's Day.*

He sat at his desk, tapping the Lamy 2000 fountain pen against a lined pad of paper. The cigar in the ashtray was nearly down to the wrapper. His escape was choreographed to the minute. His flight would be airborne before anyone was the wiser.

He looked at the clock again. 5:35 p.m. His timing was consistent. He arrived at the office before 6:00 a.m., took no more than forty-five minutes for lunch, and left at 6:00 p.m. That precision had earned trust. Predictability made people comfortable. It also made them blind.

Shawn grabbed his coat and headed for the door. As he passed each desk, he nodded and smiled, responding to greetings with polite warmth. This was his final performance. Two more days, and Michael Buster would be dead, killed in a tragic crash on the way to the office Christmas party. In truth, he would be flying south before the sirens reached the wreck.

He made his way toward the elevators, heels echoing on polished marble, but stopped to speak with Rebecca.

"Good afternoon, Rebecca," he said. "I see the invitations are coming along well. Don't stay too long."

She looked up from her desk, dark eyes lighting up. "Absolutely, Mr. Buster. Everyone's excited about the office party. Will you be joining us?"

There was a pause. Just long enough to cover what he was really thinking. Rebecca was a striking Colombian brunette who'd shared more than one after-hours drink with him. She never asked questions. He smiled. The mask fit perfectly.

"I wouldn't miss it for the world."

He stopped to shake hands and inquire about the health of his family members. He complimented someone's haircut, kissed cheeks, and remembered names. They loved that about him. What they didn't know was that he looked down on all of them.

At the elevator lobby, the indicator chimed. The doors opened. He stepped inside alone. A moment later, Jason entered from the thirty-fourth floor.

Jason was tall and awkward, barely twenty-two. The type who always looked nervous in a suit.

"Good afternoon, Mr. Buster," Jason said.

Shawn gave him a quick smile. "I reviewed those reports you sent. Excellent work."

Jason blinked, then smiled widely. "Thank you, Mr. Buster. That means a lot."

Shawn nodded, already thinking about the jet fuel receipt in his inside pocket. *Will the kid recognize my name on the news? Probably not.*

The elevator stopped at floor seventeen. Three middle-aged men stepped in, joking about eggnog and karaoke disasters. Shawn laughed with them, playing along.

"I hear the buzz about the party's building," he said.

They laughed and nodded. Harmless small talk. The kind that evaporates the moment you walk away.

When they reached the ground level, Shawn stepped out first. He walked the short corridor that led to the garage, his jaw clenched. *Thank God I won't be at that party.*

The plan was clean. A homeless man who trusted him, someone he'd fed beers and bills for weeks. The man lived under an overpass and begged by the stoplight three blocks away. Shawn had gifted him a watch and a ring, calling it a blessing. The guy cried.

He would take the wheel of Shawn's McLaren. A nameless body waiting to be claimed by fire with no apparent family or friends.

The man would get drunk and drive. The car, rigged with an incendiary device, would ignite on impact.

By the time the emergency crews arrived, the body would be beyond recognition.

A twist of nausea he hadn't expected crept into Shawn's gut.

What if this isn't as clean as I thought? What if something feels off?

He gritted his teeth. No. He had accounted for everything. *No one disappears better than I do.*

In its reserved parking space, the McLaren gleamed under the halogen lights. Silver, low-slung, and clinical. It was the most expensive car Shawn could find. He loved how it made him feel about himself.

He slid into the seat and started the engine. The growl dropped to a controlled hum. As the garage gate lifted, he eased out onto the street without looking back.

Shawn was already gone before anyone noticed he'd left.

CHAPTER 5:
GHOST CHASE

15 April 2010, 0813 hours
Tangi Valley, Wardak Province, Afghanistan, near
Ghazni base

The convoy rolled into Tangi Valley just after 0800 hours. Their mission was to capture or kill Asadullah Rahim Bakshi, known as Ghost One, a local Taliban commander moving covertly toward Kabul.

Everyone in the three-vehicle patrol wore civilian clothes, mostly black or brown, standard for Special Forces operating in the region. The terrain resembled the eastern Sierra Nevada foothills: harsh, uneven, and scattered with jagged outcrops. Spring had arrived, but the air remained cold, holding around fifty degrees. Rain from the night before had soaked the ground, leaving dirt roads slick and the air heavy with the scent of wet earth.

In the trail vehicle, Major Edward "Eddy" Kevin Ludt sat silently, adjusting the strap on his vest. The convoy consisted of three up-armored Humvees. Captain Douglas, leading from the front vehicle, crackled over the radio.

"Alright, listen up. We need to capture some Taliban if we can. We need fresh intel."

Sergeant Charley Hadderton, the commander's driver, was the youngest at twenty-six. Pudgy and baby-faced, he looked more like a recruit than a combat-tested soldier.

In the back seat sat Captain Douglas's NCOIC, Sergeant First Class Doreman. At six-foot-six and rail-thin, he towered over the rest of the team.

The fourth man in the vehicle was their linguist, Bismillah Khan Mohammadi. A native Pashtun, he was forty-three with deep-set dark eyes, long hair, and a full beard. He blended effortlessly with the locals.

Doreman broke the silence.

"I don't know about this Major Ludt guy, sir," he said. "I've caught him talking to himself. Hell, sometimes arguing with himself. Always got his nose in a book or blasting audiobooks. Either he's quiet as a corpse or he won't shut up."

Captain Douglas didn't hesitate. "He's alright. Intel guys are all weird, and Ludt is no exception. But he delivers. You get him talking, and he says he's a scuba bum. Won't shut up about it. 'Over two hundred dives in the Barrier Reef, Belize, Guam, Okinawa...' So yeah, he's weird, but the intel he's fed us these past few months has been gold."

Douglas paused. "You hear about his battalion commander? A real nightmare. He hates her."

The sound of semiautomatic weapons' fire interrupted the casual conversation. Rounds were ricocheting off the Humvees and striking the ground. It was loud, but the rounds were coming from far enough way that the people in the convoy could still hear. At first it was unclear where the rounds were coming from, but it became apparent that they were coming from the east. The attackers chose well; the natural barrier of the sun would make them harder to spot.

"Sir, we're taking fire from the ridgeline to the east! Looks like about a dozen of them, as far as I can tell," Staff Sergeant Mark O'Hagan said over the radio.

Douglas didn't answer. He checked his M4 and sidearm, trembling with adrenaline, fingers twitching like he'd immersed them in freezing water.

"Get the fuck out and kill those bastards on the ridge!" he barked. "Try to grab one alive if you can. O'Hagan, hold security and call this in. Doreman, Tobbs, Listow, you're with me."

The Humvees ground to a halt.

Captain Douglas picked up the handset for the radio and yelled into it. "Major Ludt, sir! You're acclimated. I need you to chase that Taliban heading into the tree line while we take care of the action here. He's moving toward the junkyard. Delcey, go with him. Try to get one alive."

"You got this, sir," O'Hagan called out. "Just like Fort Hood."

O'Hagan had seen combat in Desert Storm. Ludt had not. He'd never fired a round in anger, not even in Iraq during the 2003 invasion. Only targets on a range.

"Don't make me come save your ass," O'Hagan added with a grin. "You're my battle buddy, but I'm too old for this shit."

Sergeant Delcey hadn't moved. Something was wrong.

Ludt shook with fear but masked it with sarcasm. "I'll run on ahead. Catch up if you can, Delcey. See you at the finish line."

A round cracked nearby. Ludt jumped and half-yelled, half-screamed, "Whoa!"

"Run, you fucking idiot!" O'Hagan barked.

The pencil-pushing Eddy Ludt sprinted forward, weighed down by armor and gear, his M4 ready and his M9 across his chest. He was fast but graceless.

Delcey's seatbelt jammed. He yanked out a spring knife and slashed through the strap. Climbing out, he slipped in mud and ducked behind the Humvee as two rounds cracked near his boots. The delay cost him two minutes, followed by a string of curses that could've filled every page of the green waterproof notebook in his cargo pocket.

The drivers repositioned the Humvees behind a crumbling building. The terrain made driving pointless. This was now a fight on foot.

Bizzy, the linguist, stayed back with the security team. He could run down insurgents if needed, but that wasn't his role.

Staff Sergeant Henry Dodge, the team's designated marksman, set up his MK 12 SPR. He was twenty-eight, short and skinny, barely 130 pounds, with a strong Kentucky accent.

The others formed a perimeter using the Humvees for cover. The Taliban patrol had at least a dozen fighters, most already hidden behind rocks and brush.

Dodge fired. A red mist bloomed one hundred meters out. One enemy down. He fired again but missed. The rest had disappeared.

Delcey recovered and charged uphill like a man possessed. Mud sprayed from his boots as he surged through the brush, cutting across the slope to close the gap.

AK fire rattled in the distance—three M4 shots followed quickly: two in rapid succession, then a final round.

Eddy moved as best he could. He'd never been very coordinated. Adrenaline rushed inside of him. A freedom fighter seemed to pop out of nowhere to Eddy's left, about twenty meters away. He looked just as surprised to see Eddy as Eddy was to see him. The man aimed his weapon quickly but poorly. A few rounds were fired from the man's AK-47, but no rounds hit close to Eddy.

Eddy stopped, dropped to one knee just as in training, and squeezed off three rounds accurately. The man fell backwards.

Double tap to the chest, one to the head. Just like training. I can't believe I just shot that guy! Better keep moving!

Eddy kept moving.

He pushed through the thicket and caught sight of movement. A fighter, crouched behind a rusted barrel, opened fire wildly. Ludt dove aside, dropped to one knee, raised his optic, and fired three precise rounds.

Slow is smooth, and smooth is fast. Yeah, easier said than done, like telling people to stay calm during a hijacking.

The rounds pierced the barrel. The insurgent collapsed, motionless, before his body hit the dirt.

Eddy's chest burned, but fear pushed him forward. He scanned ahead with binoculars. Movement. Someone stumbling over rocks, staying low. Eddy estimated the distance to be 150 meters.

Then he saw him. White beard. Glasses. Older. Another man carried his gear.

The younger one climbed into a blue Nissan. The older one paused to use a phone.

That's him. That's Ghost One.

Eddy jogged forward, breath ragged.

A round hit the stock of his M4. He turned and fired toward the ridgeline, but the weapon jammed. He followed his training: SPORTS—slap, pull, observe, release, tap, squeeze. Another shot cracked, hitting the upper receiver and splintering it. Eddy dropped the wrecked rifle and ran.

"Shit!" he yelled, hearing brush thrash behind him. He glanced back. Delcey was closing in fast, angling toward him from twenty meters out.

"That's Ghost One, heading for the junkyard! We gotta get him!" Ludt shouted.

He drew his M9A1, flipped it to fire, and charged.

They called it the junkyard, though it wasn't technically. Over a dozen ruined vehicles lay scattered across the clearing, most damaged in a previous artillery barrage.

A shot cracked near his boots. He flinched and squeezed.

The hammer dropped. The shot rang out by accident. It was his first negligent discharge.

Embarrassment hit hard. People get GOMORs[1] for that.

He felt disoriented and barely standing. Like so many other things in this life, I tripped into this.

---

1   **GOMOR:** General Officer Memorandum of Reprimand. A formal written reprimand issued by a General Officer (typically a one-star or above). It can be: Administrative (filed locally): Only seen by the command—doesn't follow the soldier. Permanent: Goes in the Army Military Human Resource Record—and can end a career.

CHAPTER 6:
A BAD MAN RUNS

Thursday, 25 December 2014, 0800 hours
Delta Airlines ticket counter, DFW Airport

A redhead stood in the first-class line, shifting her weight from foot to foot with impatient energy. Shawn noticed the tight jeans and the tired face and filed both away. *Details matter.*

Shawn, standing just ahead of her, glanced back casually and offered a sympathetic smile. "Tough morning?"

She sighed. "Uber was late, then kept getting lost. I overslept too."

He nodded. "One of those days."

They chatted casually as the line moved forward. Her guard softened. Shawn's tone stayed light, conversational, and disarming.

"I'm Shawn," he said, his handshake confident, the smile just shy of charming.

"Anna Maria. Where are you flying?"

"Peru. I work with a nonprofit down there. Been in finance the last ten years."

She raised an eyebrow. "That's a big change."

"I needed purpose," he said. "And distance."

Anna Maria looked down for a moment. "I'm headed to the beach. Finally divorced. Trying to remember who I was before."

He gave a supportive smile. "Good for you. You deserve it."

"I booked a small hotel nearby. Nothing fancy."

"I'm at the Marriott on the beach. They had some last-minute cancellations. You might like it better."

She hesitated. "If I cancel before three, I won't get charged. I might take a look."

"You should. This is your time now."

"I finally have control of my money," she added. "And my life."

Shawn's smile didn't fade. His eyes slid over her purse, the polished nails, the gold watch. *All useful.*

"I'll be tied up until six," he said. "Meetings, calls, checking in with my mom. But after that, maybe I can show you around?" He hesitated thoughtfully as if weighing whether to say more. "I've been divorced too. Counseling helped more than I expected."

"Next!" the Delta agent called.

Shawn gave Anna Maria a parting nod and rolled his bags forward. "Merry Christmas, ma'am. How's your day so far?"

The agent, whose name tag said "Nelly," smiled. She didn't seem hurried. A coffee sat beside her.

"I knew a Nelly once," Shawn continued. "Not as pretty though."

She smirked. "Place your bags up one at a time, please."

Shawn complied. He leaned in a little. "The woman behind me just went through a brutal divorce. I've been sharing my own story. I'm a minister, and I'd like to sit with her if possible. I think she needs a kind voice." He said it with steady conviction, a tone he had perfected over years of pretending to care.

Nelly's eyebrows rose slightly. "A minister, huh? You promise to behave?"

"I don't lie," Shawn said, voice firm. "Not to God. Not to anyone."

Anna Maria stepped forward as Nelly asked, "You OK sitting next to Casanova here?"

She smiled faintly. "As long as he doesn't quote scripture the whole time."

"OK," Nelly replied. "Gate D34." They were assigned seats 2A and 2B.

In the lounge, Shawn ordered top-shelf drinks, paying out of pocket. She watched him, curious but at ease. "So how does a Christian justify drinking?"

Shawn swirled his glass. "God made good things for us. If it brings joy without harm, why deny it?"

The loudspeaker announced Delta Flight 156 to Miami.

"Finish up. Let's go," Shawn said, downing his drink.

On the plane, their conversation flowed. He made her laugh. He touched her hand just enough to build trust. His eyes drifted toward her purse whenever she turned to the window. Eventually, she fell asleep.

He gently spread a blanket over her and quietly unzipped the side pocket of her purse. From it, he slid out a credit card and her ID with practiced hands. *One clean card. Just enough to cover my tracks before I vanish.*

At Miami International, they collected their luggage and took a shuttle to the Marriott. Shawn tipped the bellhop generously and moved with purpose.

"Check this out," he said as they entered the suite. "Just fifty bucks more than your place. But this one? It feels like a fresh start."

Anna Maria hesitated. "It feels like a splurge."

As she stepped outside for a cigarette, Shawn walked to the front desk.

"Merry Christmas. You stuck working today?" he asked the clerk.

The man, clean-cut and alert, replied, "Yes, sir. My name's Gustavo. How can I help you?"

"I need to switch the room billing from Shawn Lejune to Anna Maria Haywood. She's my fiancée, and she offered to cover it."

Gustavo frowned. "That's not standard policy. We usually keep the original name on file."

"She's outside taking a smoke break. PTSD, long story. We're staying separately for religious reasons. I maxed out my card booking this trip, so we agreed she'd cover the hotel."

Gustavo hesitated. "I might need to check with a supervisor."

Shawn gestured to the window. "There she is. See?" Anna Maria waved back.

Gustavo paused, then nodded. "Alright. We can make the change."

"God bless you," Shawn said, reaching for the man's hand. "Let me say a prayer for you."

Gustavo looked uneasy. "I don't think that's necessary."

"I'm ordained. I promise this won't take long." He closed his eyes. "Father, bless this kind soul. Let him feel your love and favor for helping a couple in need."

Shawn opened his eyes just as Anna Maria returned.

"Could I get a beach towel?" he asked. "And here's cash for sunscreen and a bottle of water."

He turned back to Anna Maria. "You've earned some peace. Change clothes, head to the beach, and spend this." He handed her two hundred dollars. "You deserve to feel like yourself again."

She hesitated. "I should probably take my wallet."

"Don't risk it. Leave it here with Gustavo. He'll lock it up."

She looked between the two men. "You're very kind," she said.

Shawn handed her belongings to Gustavo. Anna Maria headed toward the elevator with the towel in her arms.

Shawn watched her go, calm and satisfied. *Well, that was easy.*

CHAPTER 7:
COVERT FLIGHT PLANS

Thursday, 25 December 2014, 1400 hours
Shawn's room at the Marriott Hotel, Miami, Florida

In his hotel room, Shawn thought things through for one whole minute, then he slid a new SIM card into his burner phone and made the call.

"Hey, Johnny. Merry Christmas, man. It's Shawn Lejune. I need a private flight from Miami to Lima. Quiet, no checks. Talk to your people—Peru's a mess. Medical supplies disappear unless you grease the right palms. If I'm going to help anyone, this medicine needs to make it through untouched. I'll pay in soles. Makes things smoother."

"OK, but remember it's Christmas, dude. Give me a few days," Johnny replied.

Johnny Croenen sat with a fat dip of Wintergreen Skoal in his cheek. He was an athletic man in his forties, a former infantryman and Army sniper who'd later become a drill sergeant. After eight years, he walked away to fly planes for a living.

He had a rough face from years of bar fights and busted knuckles. Mostly German blood. Heavy drinker. Hated reading but loved the outdoors and roaring down highways on his Harley. Twice divorced, two kids, and a lifestyle he could barely afford. These jobs gave him a rush. They also kept the bills paid.

Shawn leaned closer to the phone. "I need to be in Peru before New Year's Day. From Lima, it'll take a couple of days to get where I'm going with the way the roads are. I'll make it worth your while. Gold, off the books. And five grand more if you can get me out in the next two days. Gold Krugerrands, Johnny. The most recognized coin in the world. No middlemen. Just you."

Flatter the moron and he'll comply, Shawn thought. I need to offload some of these Krugerrands anyway—too much weight.

There was a pause on the other end. Shawn heard keys tapping.

Two minutes later, Johnny said, "Alright. I can do Saturday the 27th. Sooners not possible. Plane needs maintenance."

Shawn kept the charm flowing. "You're the man, Johnny. I knew I could count on you. I have two security personnel accompanying me. I'll text you their info on this number only. After this call, I'm ditching this line."

"So mysterious, as always," Johnny said, his voice thick with sarcasm.

"You have no idea, my friend," Shawn replied. He quickly texted the names of the two ex-Special Forces men he'd hired. Both were from the 7th Group. Fluent in Spanish. Experienced in South America.

Then he removed the SIM card, dropped it in a ceramic bowl, and microwaved it for a minute. After it sparked and died, he crushed what was left with a spoon and flushed it.

Shawn sat back in silence, already picturing how the next phase would unfold.

A knock came at the door.

It was Anna Maria, wrapped in a white towel and a yellow bikini. Skin bronzed just short of burning.

Too bad I'm working.

She draped the towel over a bamboo chair. "I've had enough sun for one day."

"Hey, babe. How're you doing?" Shawn asked. "What do you say we hit the hot tub downstairs, then grab dinner? It's on me. I only have the room for two nights and then I need to check out and be on my way."

Anna Maria smiled. "Well... maybe. As friends."

Shawn shrugged. "God expects us to enjoy ourselves."

$$$$$

On the morning of December 27th, Shawn was already in the hotel gym, going through his routine.

She won't notice the missing card. Not yet.

Back in the room, he showered, dressed, and began packing his suitcase. Right on cue, he heard Anna Maria's familiar knock.

She looked exhausted. It was only 0800. "I don't know how you do it, Shawn," she said.

The drugs help.

"Oh well, early bird gets the worm," he replied with a cheerful grin. "Feel free to hang out, order room service for breakfast. Charge it to the room." *You're the one paying for it, after all.*

She thanked him.

"Don't mention it. The Lord tells us to be cheerful givers. By the way, have you thought about those church groups I told you about?"

Anna Maria hesitated. "I don't know, Shawn. That stuff's not really for me. But since you're such a gentleman, I promise I'll give it a try."

Shawn gave her a firm look. "Once you're close to the Lord, Anna, you won't want to go back."

He closed his suitcase. "I'm all packed. I'll catch a cab downstairs." He kissed her on the cheek, hoping she'd stay in, rack up some charges, and not notice any alerts until he was long gone.

"Bye, Shawn!" she called after him.

CHAPTER 8:
SHAWN HEADS TO PERU

Saturday, 27 December 2014, 1900 hours
Johnny Croenen's private airplane hangar, Miami
International Airport

Johnny Croenen and his copilot girlfriend, Mariami Morales, helped load the duffel bags and five crates into the Learjet 36A. The aircraft was just big enough for Shawn, his two hired guns, the flight crew, and their gear.

Shawn had met Johnny the day before and paid in gold, which Johnny verified at a local pawn shop. He and Mariami were ready to disappear into Belize, where taxes, alimony, and other burdens would no longer follow them.

As they waited for the others to arrive, Shawn went to sleep on a cot with the assistance of some sleep meds. He woke up at 0530, conducted his personal hygiene routine, and ate snacks he'd brought. At 0617, two rough-looking men showed up with their own bags. Shawn nodded at them and instructed them to set their bags in the corner.

Johnny, Shawn, and the two men gathered in Johnny's corner hangar, converted into a briefing lounge with chairs, dry-erase boards, and wooden tables. They had time to talk before departure. Johnny knew the two men were security for Shawn, and they didn't bother to introduce themselves. They gave him a nod, which he reciprocated.

Takeoff was scheduled for 7:30 a.m., and it was now 6:25 a.m. Mariami stepped out to conduct the final checks while Johnny opened his notes.

"Look, Shawn," Johnny said. "I don't care what's in your cargo, but if we want to get through customs, we need to stay coordinated. And we can't pay these guys in gold. They won't even know if it's real."

"I told you, I have soles," Shawn replied. "Smuggling these medical supplies is more complicated than moving coke. Everyone wants a cut. But this should cover it."

He pulled a small black bag from under his seat. When he unzipped it, thirty thousand soles in 100-sol notes were stacked neatly inside; the equivalent of $10,572. "Use this. I don't want anyone searching us or our bags."

The two men with Shawn were clearly mercenaries. Their tattoos marked past deployments, their bodies lean and hardened by experience. One wore coyote brown cargo pants, the other black. Both wore dark sunglasses, cheap digital watches, and no jewelry. Nothing that would catch the wrong kind of attention. The taller of the two was Frederico Ramirez: the other, Manuel Flores.

Johnny ran through his flight brief until Mariami returned. His dark brown eyes sparkled when they met hers, knowing freedom and a life without debt were just hours away.

He turned to Shawn and his crew. "Any questions? If not, let's load up. Relax during the flight. Just don't argue with anyone at the airport, and everything will go smoothly. Once you clear customs, I'm out. You're on your own."

No one said a word. They nodded and headed to the jet.

Twenty minutes later, the jet lifted off. Shawn raised a glass of Jack Daniels and toasted the shrinking buildings below. The flight to Peru was smooth and uneventful.

They arrived feeling refreshed after the seven-hour flight. At Lima's Jorge Chávez International Airport, Johnny stepped outside to meet a customs contact. They had arranged this in advance. The official accepted two bottles of Jack Daniels and the bag of thirty thousand soles. Johnny cracked his knuckles, nervous yet hopeful that the bribe would work.

The process took less than thirty minutes. Shawn and his two hired guns were driven by private car to the calm and upscale district of Miraflores. The coastal neighborhood reminded Shawn of Santa Barbara: temperate, clean, and deceptively serene.

They checked into the oceanfront Marriott. Shawn had prepaid for the rooms using Anna Maria's credit card. They would spend the night here and depart at 5:00

a.m. for the ten-hour journey to Huancayo, with several planned stops along the way.

The time was 4:25 p.m. They ordered an early dinner and planned to get a good night's sleep. Later, at 7:00 p.m., a massage service would arrive, booked from one of the city's less reputable directories. Shawn opened his bag, pulled out another bottle of Jack Daniels', poured himself a drink, and thought about the future.

CHAPTER 9:
THE CHASE BEGINS

Monday, 12 January 2015, 1100 hours
Office of Carlos Ortiz, CEO, Trufunds headquarters,
Dallas, Texas

It was a beautiful office with a plush blue carpet, the kind your shoes sank into. Seated around the polished conference table were the executive members of Trufunds Bank.

At the head sat Carlos Ortiz, a first-generation Mexican American who had clawed his way to the top. His self-indulgent lifestyle was beginning to catch up with him. Carlos stood five feet, five inches, with thick black glasses and hair untouched by gray, despite his sixty years. His crumpled suit and slumped posture didn't help his image. In his hand was a clear glass of double scotch whiskey with two ice cubes, his drink of choice.

To Carlos's right sat Tommy Chong, head of security, an Asian American with a rigid posture and drumming fingers. Deep creases in his forehead and a clenched jaw made his irritation evident.

Next to Tommy was Regina Kline, the acting Chief Financial Officer, temporarily filling in after Michael Buster's spectacular downfall. Over the holidays, Buster had died in a car crash, but not before stealing over ten million dollars through wire transfers and cryptocurrency.

Regina, an attractive Black woman from Jamaica, was a relentless workaholic. She carried her efficiency into every part of her life, even her wardrobe—no jewelry, just sharp, tailored pantsuits built for performance, not fashion.

To Carlos's left sat Cecilia Herrera, head of cybersecurity, a Hispanic woman in her mid-forties with a slender frame and reserved smile. She dressed professionally, but never in a flashy way. Her tidy appearance mirrored the precision she brought to her work.

The final person in the room was Diane Ferry. Once Tommy's girlfriend, she now looked anything but comfortable. She sat across from him stiffly, like a student caught cheating. Her eyes stayed fixed on the conference table, avoiding the accusing stares around her. She wore a modest white dress, pearl earrings, and matching shoes.

Carlos started the meeting, his voice slicing through the silence.

"Let me get this straight, Diane," he said, voice rising. "You gave Michael Buster access codes to my office and computer because he needed to get something done faster?" He laughed bitterly. "My God, you absolute idiot. You give a whole new meaning to the word 'bimbo'." He slammed his whiskey glass on the table. "Tell me you didn't actually believe him."

Diane was already crying. "Yes, I believed him. He said he had a new algorithm that would generate more revenue for the company and its clients. He said you'd push back unless you saw it was working."

Carlos glared at her, too angry to speak.

Tommy pinched the bridge of his nose and exhaled through clenched teeth. His other hand tapped the table. "Carlos, ripping into Diane isn't going to fix this. The damage is done. We need to clean it up. Now."

Ortiz took a long pull from his glass. "Fine. Diane, that'll be all. Security will walk you to your desk to collect your things. Turn in your badge and leave the building." He paused, voice sharpening. "And don't forget your nondisclosure agreement."

Tommy nodded to one of the guards, who started for the door, motioning for Diane to follow.

She left sobbing.

Carlos turned to Tommy. "We have bigger problems. Buster stole something I can't exactly report."

Tommy frowned. "What do you mean?"

Carlos leaned forward. "I used client funds for crypto. It was a sure thing until Buster stole my key." He paused. "The only thing that kept him from cleaning me out is Cecilia's security patch. It's just a matter of time. The police can't find out."

Tommy looked at Carlos with disgust and leaned back, thinking. "We need outside help."

"I was afraid you'd say that," Carlos muttered. "What do you have in mind?"

Tommy tapped the table. "My nephew. Former Army Ranger. Works for a private firm called Silent Wolf now. They pull from Army Special Forces, Navy SEALs, Marine Force Recon, and Air Force Special Operations to include: Combat Control (CCT), Pararescue (PJ), Tactical Air Control Party (TACP), and Tactical Operations (TACOPS). He's expensive, but he gets results. We won't officially use Silent Wolf. He takes personal jobs sometimes."

Carlos sighed. "Fine. Do it. Just keep it quiet."

Tommy nodded. "I'll call him tonight."

$$\$\$\$\$\$\$$$

Later that evening, Tommy made another call.

"Hey, Angie. It's Tommy. How's David? Still playing softball?"

Angelina Vasquez sighed. "Tommy, I don't have time for small talk. What do you want?"

"I need a favor."

Silence stretched between them. Tommy heard Angie's fingers drum against a hard surface.

"Tommy, I can't risk my pension."

"You don't have to. Just... investigate something for me."

She hesitated. "This isn't legal, is it?"

"Do you really want to ask me that?" Tommy's voice softened. "You trust me, right?"

"Fine. But this is the last time."

Tommy chuckled. That's what you said last time, Angie.

"OK, this is what I need..." He spent five minutes explaining, drawing on his experience in law enforcement.

After the call, Angie hung up. Tommy knew she already regretted her decision. But regret wouldn't pay bills, and Tommy offered her a way out of the bureaucratic maze she'd been stuck in at the Dallas PD for years. Dangerous, but a way out, nonetheless. Whatever Tommy needed, Angie would find it. He was sure of it.

CHAPTER 10:
COLD TRAILS, HOT LEADS

Tuesday, 13 January 2015, 1900 hours
Office of Angelina Vasquez, Dallas Police Department,
Dallas, Texas

Angie waited until the neighborhood had settled into its usual winter hush. She pulled the burner phone from her desk drawer and pressed Tommy's number.

Tommy Chong, tired, answered on the second ring. "Hello?"

"It's Angie," she said, sounding just as worn out.

"Well, you didn't call to ask how I'm doing. What do you have for me?" His tone made it clear he wasn't in the mood to play twenty questions.

Angie rolled her eyes. "No, Tommy. You know me better than that. I checked it out, just like you asked. And yeah, you were right to be suspicious."

He sighed. "This suspense is killing me. What did you find?"

Angie smiled. Tommy always got testy when he was on the outside looking in.

"The case looked clean on the surface, but something felt off. I've been with Dallas PD for twenty-eight years. I know when something doesn't sit right. The setup, burn severity, and missing ID matched two older cases I recall from my time in uniform. Solo crashes. Both happened on I-35. One in '94, Shawn Larson. One in '01, Shawn McFadden. Same crash type. Expensive cars. Bodies burned beyond recognition. Both cases closed fast. And now there's another. Same stretch of road. Same conditions. All three victims were the same age at their time of death."

"I've never heard those names, Angie. They don't mean anything to me. A lot of people that age die in crashes on I-35, unfortunately."

"McFadden's case was reopened last month. Larson's followed a week later. Turns out he had ties to organized crime. His sudden death, maxed-out credit cards, and the theft of his rich girlfriend's house two days before he died raised too many red flags.

"There was one photograph of Shawn Larson at a party that made the news. One of our detectives is in the Army Reserves and recognized the man standing next to him."

She pulled out a newspaper clipping from Arlington, Texas. Several men in their mid-twenties sat at a Republican Party fundraiser.

"There's Shawn." She pointed, though she knew Tommy couldn't see it. "And his friend, Eddy Ludt." She tapped on a smaller man in the picture, sitting on Shawn's right, who was not as confident but had an intelligent look. Both men wore blue suits with blue ties. Beers sat on the table in front of them.

Tommy was quiet. "I assume you'll send me a copy of the photos you're referring to?"

Angie ignored him. *Of course, I'll send them.* "You know that church group that just came under scrutiny? Luz del Redentor Internacional?"

"Yes."

"The name of the church in English is Light of the Redeemer International. Shawn Michael Larson helped start it. It's based in Peru. The feds believe it's being used to launder money. Buster's million-dollar policy went to that church.

"Shawn McFadden and Michael Buster were major donors to the organization. They were also ordained ministers. Their cases were reassigned to the same cold case detective," she continued. "While going through the files, he noticed a handwriting quirk in McFadden's checks. The curved y's, the pressure points. He sent the samples to an expert and ran them through FISH[2]."

"And?"

"Ninety-eight percent match. Same hand in both cases. Then, I pulled Buster's HR documents and ran those. Same result."

She paused.

"Meet me at HaruSakura," Tommy said. "Tomorrow. Six."

---

2   **FISH:** Forensic Information System for Handwriting.

CHAPTER 11:
TOMMY WINES AND DINES ANGIE

Wednesday, 14 January 2015, 1800 hours
HaruSakura Sushi & Ramen House, Plano, Texas

Angie entered HaruSakura and headed to Tommy's table. He was seated in the back booth, the food waiting: two spicy tuna rolls, gyoza, and a tall Asahi. Angie sat down,

opened her tablet and got to the point before Tommy was able to say anything. "Buster, McFadden, Larson. Different names, same pattern, same man." Angie handed him the tablet.

Tommy scrolled through the files. "Nice to see you too, Angie. The deaths all followed the same pattern."

"Exactly," she said. "Crash. Burned body, everything burned to a crisp. Everyone assumes he's dead. In McFadden's case, his girlfriend swears he stole the jewelry before the crash. She still believes he faked his death and took off with it. In addition to the handwriting, Larson and McFadden shared a t-shaped scar on their left arms, just like the one Buster had."

Tommy had noticed that same scar. Buster said he got it skiing. *Who knows, maybe he did.* "How did you know about the scars?"

"I saw college photos of Shawn Larson playing intramural sports and attending fraternity events," Angie explained. "Shawn Larson ran a business getting motels and hotels discounts on their utility bills, and he took some publicity photos with happy clients."

They both exchanged knowing looks. He nodded. It was time to let Angie in on more of the story.

Tommy reached into his coat and slid a folded sheet across the table. "Over five million dollars gone. One morning, the books were clean. That afternoon, everything had been moved—wire transfers, offshore layering, phantom vendors. It happened very quickly," he said, neglecting to mention Carlos's illegal gambling.

Angie read through the report, then looked up. "You've already started."

"I hired contractors. They're quiet and they don't ask questions. They've got a direction, and I've given them orders to recover him alive." *But if he dies after we get what we need, no skin off my nose.*

"*If* they get him," Angie said, "he comes to my station. No calls ahead. No special handling."

Tommy nodded. "You'll have him." He pulled out a nice leather purse from his bag.

Her eyes drifted to the purse. "Early retirement gift?"

"A thank-you," he said. "And a placeholder. When you're done with the badge in what, nine months?"

"Ten, but who's counting?"

"When the time comes, we'd like you at Trufunds. Compliance, internal risk. The kind of work you're already good at, just quieter."

Angie smirked. "I'm still on duty. And this case is active." *And I'm not done yet.*

"I know." Tommy knew there were limits to what Angie would do for him, and he wasn't going to push her any further.

CHAPTER 12:
HELP FROM A FRIEND IN NEED WHO IS NOT A FRIEND INDEED

Thursday, 8 January 2015, 0825 hours
Eddy's house, Grapevine, Texas

Eddy sat in his small house in Grapevine, Texas. It was just the right size, small enough to manage. The place was older than he was, but he didn't care. He'd scored a deal near shops and the old-style railway.

His washer and dryer sat in the living and dining area. The house had only two small bedrooms, one bathroom, and a garage for his sports car.

The yard was approximately ten by fifteen feet, providing space for his dog to stretch her legs between walks.

He was practical, not artistic. The walls had no pictures, only a few mirrors. His firearms were stashed throughout the house.

Eddy had a civilian job, but he was what they called a BURB, basically an Unemployed Reserve Bum. He spent more time on Army Reserve duty than at work. He was between tours and back at Ultimate Flights, stuck doing IT work again. Bored out of his mind, he was already running late after fiddling with his scuba gear, prepping it for another week-long dive trip to Nassau.

He rushed out the door to his Kona Blue 2012 Ford Mustang, a car that represented everything he wasn't. Cool, athletic, powerful. It roared to life. The models from the '80s and '90s never appealed to him; they were too much like go-karts. But when the newer ones hit the market in 2004, he finally took notice. Even then, Eddy, ever the penny-pincher, waited until he "needed" a car before buying the 2012 Mustang. He had hoped some of Steve McQueen's coolness would rub off on him.

Fat chance, Eddy.

Pursuing that fantasy, he sped to work, somehow avoiding a speeding ticket and making it in one piece.

He pulled into the parking lot just in time and rushed to his cubicle on the second floor. From reservations to IT, he now codes at the airline's headquarters. It was a job that bored him stiff. He was never at work long enough to become an expert in anything due to his frequent Army tours.

Rosa Lemoria, his boss, loathed him for no apparent reason. He guessed that she resented that his military service allowed him to accumulate time with the company.

"Hey Rosa, how was your Christmas? I'll get those reports to you soon, don't worry."

Rosa forced a smile that didn't reach her eyes. "Don't you have another reserve tour to leave for? Fix your shirt." Then, rolling her eyes, she added, "Do you get dressed in the dark?"

The holidays were over; no need to pretend to like him anymore.

He ignored her comment about his reserve tour and stayed expressionless, knowing that nothing he said would change her attitude. *Fuck off*, he thought.

What've I done to deserve such a rude boss?

$$\text{\small s\$\$\$\$ss}$$

After work, Eddy thought about his upcoming dive trip. Five nights and six days on a boat. He hadn't dived in the Bahamas yet.

His phone rang. Expecting his friend Pierre Bernard, he answered the call. But instead of Pierre's voice, Eddy heard someone he hadn't spoken to in ten years, a voice he never wanted to hear again.

"Hey, buddy! Happy belated New Year! It's Shawn. How've you been? Look, I know we had a falling out, but I want to make amends with you. Go check your mailbox. There's $200,000 cash in a metal box. It's a down payment on your soon-to-be retirement."

Eddy tensed. Years ago, he had worked for Shawn in a private investigation firm that made a fortune before going bankrupt to dodge taxes. Shawn had used the company to launder money. Eddy was just the tech nerd, the information systems guy.

He shook his head in irritation. *Are you kidding me?* But still, the temptation of money gnawed at him. Against his better judgment, his feet carried him outside.

He was about to end the call when Shawn interrupted.

"Don't hang up."

In the background, Eddy heard a woman giggling.

Eddy said accusingly, "Shawn, first, I thought you were dead. I was questioned by the police, for crying out loud!"

Shawn responded immediately. "No, I know they thought that, but I was on a retreat in Oregon with no cell coverage or electronics allowed. I was gone for one month. My cousin was using my car, and they obviously thought it was me. It was all straightened out. I have a sweet deal for you—private jet to my villa in Peru. Easy money. Some asshole is trying to blackmail me. I need your tech skills."

Eddy hesitated.

"Where did the money come from?"

"Don't worry about that. Just say yes, bro."

There was silence for thirty seconds before Shawn added, "Think about it."

Eddy hung up on Shawn. Then, he checked the mailbox.

Sure enough, there it was, $200,000 neatly stacked.

Something was wrong. Shawn was always looking out for himself.

Do I take the money? Call the police? What's the crime? I was really looking forward to that dive.

CHAPTER 13:
CALLING A REAL FRIEND

Friday, 9 January 2015, 2000 hours
Donald's house, Miami-Dade, Florida

"Yeah, babe, I remembered to get the wine. I'd never forget the booze," Donald Delcey laughed with a wide grin.

He was an Army Reservist living on the outskirts of Tampa, Florida. His day job was teaching high school history. He coached track and field and volunteered as a Big Brother for troubled teens.

Donald had married his high school sweetheart, Pamela Sanchez, a Black Mexican woman tough as nails. Being apart from her never sat right with him. They'd wanted to escape the cold up north in Pennsylvania and go somewhere with more sunshine and less snow. Don wasn't one for getting in the water, but he loved fishing and hated the cold, so Florida felt like the obvious choice.

He'd transferred college credits earned before joining the Army to Florida State University and convinced Pamela to move with him. He got to keep his guns, and she got to paint by the water.

The phone rang. Eddy Ludt.

They'd forged a bond in Afghanistan that never would have formed otherwise. They were as different as oil and water. Donald was athletic, confident, and extroverted. He had gotten into bodybuilding and looked like a Greek god, with chiseled muscles and a strong jawline. Eddy struggled with his weight and always had to fight to stay within Army standards. He was into chess, puzzles, and reading. His only real physical outlet was scuba diving.

"What's up, dog? You keeping the airlines safe with that Browning Hi-Power?" Don grinned, referring to Eddy's favorite pistol. Eddy wasn't an operator, but he loved guns.

Now, a sergeant first class drilling with Special Operations Command Central out of MacDill Air Force Base, Donald always picked up when Eddy called.

He liked the guy.

"Well, we need to catch up, but this isn't really a social call. It's more of a call of concern. Remember that retard I'm always complaining about, the one who manipulated everyone and always got away with it?"

"Shawn? How could I forget? You bring him up all the time." Even back in college. The practical jokes. Pouring cold water on people in the shower. Smearing mayonnaise on the dorm phone. Trashing someone's car and blaming them for it. And that was just surface-level crap. "I thought you were leaving him alone."

Eddy sighed. "I was leaving Shawn alone, but he called from a number I didn't recognize. Then someone dropped two hundred grand in my mailbox. He told me to quit my job and take an all-expense-paid trip to Peru.

Now he's offering another eight hundred thousand to fix some hard key encryption linked to his cryptocurrency stash."

He paused. "I know he's not telling me everything, and let's be honest, he's stealing. No one is that generous unless they're hiding something. He cheated me constantly when I worked for him."

Donald could hear Eddy spiraling. "Look, man, think this through. As far as you know, he hasn't broken any laws. You still live in the same house. You've had the same phone number for what, fifteen years? Are you going to claim he committed a crime by putting money in your mailbox? Technically, only the postal service is allowed to use it."

"I can't take the money, Don. I can't prove it, but I know he's doing something illegal. I must go to the authorities."

Donald stayed calm. "Right now, you need to take a tactical pause. Like I said, he hasn't broken any laws you can prove. How are you even going to get that money back to him? Let me help. I'll reach out to a few people and see if there's been any chatter about him. You're an excellent analyst, but you're too emotional when it comes to Shawn."

Eddy was quiet for a moment, chewing on guilt, resentment, and something else he didn't want to name because it was too dark. "Thanks, man. I wish everyone believed in me like you do. Okay, we'll wait a few days to a week, but please call me, alright? I'm going to lose sleep over this. If he's doing something illegal, I want to report him. I want this guy caught and taken care of, once and for all. I've learned from experience that turning a blind eye to evil only makes things worse."

Donald respected that. "OK, Ed. It's Friday. I'll make some calls to my federal buddies and check in with some of the guys I trained with who're doing contract work now. There are always shady people operating off the radar. They hear things. Call me next Friday."

"Later, dude," Eddy replied, trying to sound cool and failing miserably.

CHAPTER 14:
BAR TALK

Friday, 16 January 2015, 1923 hours
Silver Gorilla Bar, Ybor City, Florida

Pete, Tommy Chong's nephew, lounged back in his chair, one arm draped over the worn chair. He was lean, muscular, and looked like he belonged in a fight.

Across from him sat Wise Dog. Everyone in the Special Forces community had a call sign, and his had stuck. He was Black, five foot nine, built like a tank at 240 pounds, and covered in tattoos that weren't just for show. They were his resume.

Airborne Wings on his right shoulder. *These Things We Do, That Others May Live* in bold blue ink down his left forearm. *Property of USAF* etched on the right.

A list of countries where he'd served: Afghanistan, Bosnia, Haiti, Iraq, Kosovo, with the years served beside each one.

But one tattoo stood out. *Hong Kong 2013* on his upper arm. Pete had always meant to ask. Tonight, he did.

"Bullshit. I'm not buying it." Pete jabbed a finger toward the tattoo. "You didn't go after Snowden."

Wise Dog sat in silence, unreadable. Then, with the calm confidence of a man who didn't explain himself, he said, "I never said I did."

Pete smirked. "All your tats mean something. You weren't on vacation."

Wise Dog shrugged. "Wise Dog tells no lies."

A whistleblower had fled to Hong Kong in 2013. Rumors swirled, but nothing was confirmed. Pete watched his friend's face. Nothing gave him away.

He changed the subject. "My uncle is paying half a million just to find one guy."

Wise Dog chuckled. "You expect me to believe that?"

"Believe what you want." Pete took a slow sip of his soda. "They want it handled before the cops catch up. It's legal, technically, but unofficial. My uncle doesn't want blowback."

Wise Dog looked up from his drink. "So, they're doing illegal activity at Trufunds, and they want mercs, not bounty hunters."

Pete exhaled. "Tommy says it's clean. But yeah, they need results."

"What's my cut? And how quiet is this?"

"You can't tell anyone, even after. Not the full story."

Wise Dog rolled his eyes. "Double secret probation?"

Pete ignored the joke. He was still fried from his flight. "We need intel. This guy travels a lot. South America. Mostly Rio. Always with some rich mistress."

Wise Dog pulled a notepad from inside his leather jacket. "Weapons? Financials? Timeline?"

"Minimal weapons. Concealed. Pistols only." Pete leaned in. "We tell people he skipped bail on cocaine and sexual assault. Make it official."

"I'll grease the right palms to make the paper trail legit. Give me a week."

Pete grinned. "I knew you wouldn't let me down."

Wise Dog drained his tonic water. He never drank alcohol when riding his Harley.

"I'll call you in a week," he said. "Don't call me unless some hot chick wants my perfect body."

Pete smirked. "I don't bother dogs when they're fighting or eating. Looks like you'll be doing both soon."

He felt it already. The tingling up his spine. The itch.

Nothing hits like a real mission. Not skydiving. Not base jumping. Not wild hogs or MMA. Combat ruined him for anything else.

And Wise Dog? He was already running the numbers.

CHAPTER 15:
WISE DOG COMES THROUGH

Saturday, 24 January 2015, 1034 hours
Alamo Wildlands hunting reserve, San Antonio, Texas

Peter Zhao's apartment in San Antonio smelled like cheap perfume and booze. His latest fling—was it Leila? Patricia? —was glaring at him. He changed women like some people changed shirts. They always disappointed him, or so he claimed.

"If I want to talk to the hot waitress, that's my business!" Pete yelled, his temper flaring.

He hurled his notebook onto the coffee table. It skidded off and hit the floor.

"Yeah? Well, you can sleep on the couch, you two-timer." The curvy Latina woman snatched up the notebook and chucked it back at him, striking his arm.

Pete smirked, puffing up his chest. "One problem, this is my house. If you don't like it, you leave."

Without another word, Leila Gonzalez grabbed her purse and stormed out. The door slammed behind her, shaking the walls.

Pete exhaled, rubbing his temple. *Good riddance.*

His phone buzzed, the familiar sound of slot machines ringing in the background. Wise Dog.

"What up, dude?" came the deep, amused voice. "Hope I interrupted something you'll regret later."

Pete kicked back on the couch, already swiping through social media, scoping out new prospects. "Not at all. We are shopping for a replacement as we speak. You're a day early. You got something, or are you just wasting my time?"

Wise Dog chuckled. "Yeah, my boy Don Delcey knows a guy. Remember the story about that Major who supposedly took down a Taliban commander with a pistol at an impossible range?"

Pete rolled his eyes. "That was bullshit. Nobody shoots like that."

"Maybe," Wise Dog said. "But Delcey says this guy, Ludt, is the real deal. He's a coder, a hacker, and apparently, our target reached out to him. Wants him to unlock a hard drive and set up a network in the mountains outside Lima, Peru."

Pete sat up. "No shit?"

"No shit," Wise Dog confirmed. "And he already got paid two hundred grand in cash, with another eight hundred promised for a month's work. He isn't going to keep the money because he knows it's dirty."

Pete's mind raced. "OK, I want to talk to this guy. Where is he?"

"Dallas Fort Worth area," replied Wise Dog.

Pete smirked. "First-class flights, VIP treatment, good food, booze, women, make sure he enjoys himself. We put him on our payroll."

"Got it. I'll call my contact," Wise Dog said, ending the call.

$$$$$$

Winston sat in a weathered chair in a wooden shack with no floor on a hunting reserve, a Marlboro between his fingers. The last of his hair clung to the sides of his head, refusing to surrender entirely. He was a dead shot and knew more about firearms than most, but he wasn't a violent man by nature. At least, not anymore. He was tired of killing people. Wild game, though? That was different.

His matte black Ruger Scout .350 Legend rested on a stand. Boars were predictable, unlike skittish deer.

Winston's phone rang. He recognized the number. Wise Dog never called at this hour, unless it was important.

"Yeah?" he answered.

"I need you to train someone," Wise Dog said. "Good money in it. No illegal shit, but we keep it under wraps. Only a few people in the inner circle."

Winston exhaled smoke. "OK, tell me more."

"You're going to get to play with a field-grade officer and tell him what to do."

Winston flicked his cigarette into the dirt. "Fine. What caliber?"

"He needs pistol training, not rifles. Let's say nine-millimeter. You're the best pistol instructor I know."

Winston scratched his chin. "Two weeks. Intensive. He trains eight hours a day, six days a week. By the time we're done, he'll either be a real shooter or he'll wish he never met me."

"That's why I called you," Wise Dog said.

"Thirty grand tax-free," Winston added. "And I keep the extra ammo."

"Done."

Winston leaned back in his chair, already planning the regimen in his head. He'd already had an adrenaline fix to last a lifetime from his years as a Federal Marshal. These days, he trains others. It was easier; less PTSD.

"Send me his specs," Winston said. "Oh, and Wise?"

"Yeah?"

"I'm better than you ever were, even on your best day."

Wise Dog chuckled. "Keep telling yourself that, old man."

The call ended.

Winston stood and stretched. He had a training plan to build and a so-called sharpshooter to break in.

CHAPTER 16:
SWALLOW YOUR PRIDE,
LURE THE PREY

Sunday, 18 January 2015, 0750 hours
Eddy's house, Grapevine, Texas

From the start, Eddy didn't trust Shawn. The guy wasn't stupid, and he sure as hell wasn't patient. That made him dangerous. Unreliable.

When Shawn wanted something, he got it.

That was why Eddy had stalled, sending a brief text back on January 4.

Eddy: I need to think about it.

Since then, Eddy had ignored Shawn's repeated calls and texts. He knew Shawn would be pissed. The man wasn't used to waiting, especially not for someone like Eddy.

Fresh out of university in 1993, Eddy was broken and desperate. He didn't have a choice. He met Shawn at the University of Texas at Arlington's Lagos Hall. Back then, Shawn had a way of charming his way into people's lives, always knowing exactly what to say.

But the charm was just another tool.

If there had been a degree in pranks and screwing around, Shawn would have graduated with honors.

Regardless, he'd landed a full-ride scholarship to the University of Pennsylvania. Things always seemed to come easily to him.

A few years later, he'd resurfaced in the Dallas–Fort Worth metroplex, still the same reckless, arrogant bastard. But now, he had money and power.

Eddy worked for him briefly, but the deeper he looked, the dirtier things got.

So, he walked away.

Unpaid.

ss$$$ss

Eddy was reading a paperback on his bed with a can of Dr. Pepper on the nightstand. His phone rang. Reaching for it, he knocked over the can, splashing soda across the nightstand and onto the floor.

He saw the incoming call from Donald while walking to the kitchen to grab a cloth.

Eddy smirked as he answered. "Hey, Don, you finally decided to go scuba diving with me?"

He knew the answer, but teasing Don about Eddy's edge at diving never got old.

Don chuckled. "Yeah, no. The only good thing about the ocean is pulling fish out of it." His tone sharpened. "I talked to some guys from Group. There's chatter about some big money if this guy is who we think he is."

Eddy rinsed the washcloth and walked back to his bedroom. "What, he won the lottery and wants to split it with us?"

His joke landed flat.

Don didn't laugh. "Well, first, he did lie to you. He'd been declared dead, with insurance paid out. He's a con artist, Eddy, a big one. Shawn Larson might be his real name, but he went by at least two aliases after that. Shawn McFadden in 1994 and then Michael Buster in 2001. Each time, a lot of money was lost or paid out in insurance to the same non-profit Christian organization 'Luz del Redentor Internacional'."

Eddy drummed his fingers against the table. That wasn't surprising. Shawn never did anything without personal gain.

"No kidding, he's not dead. He called me, for God's sake. I could have told you that. So, what's the deal? He steals from the wrong people?"

"Trufunds Bank." Don's voice was flat. "And at least one body has already dropped."

Eddy froze. That changed everything. A con was one thing. Murder was something else.

"So let me get this straight. You want me, a computer guy, to go after a killer?"

"You're missing the point, man. He came to you. That's why we can't use someone else. You already have a reason to be near him."

Eddy shook his head. "No, that's what law enforcement is for. We have these people called Federal Marshals who carry guns and get paid to do this shit."

Don sighed. "C'mon, this can't go through official channels. The bank wants its money back, and it wants it fast. Fast enough to take risks most people wouldn't touch. Pete told me his Uncle Tommy has a contact in the Dallas PD who's sniffing around. Your name came up in a newspaper photograph with Shawn."

"Yeah, I remember. Some charity fundraiser," Eddy muttered. "So, what exactly are we talking about here?"

Don hesitated. "We need someone close. Someone who can get inside. That's you."

Silence.

Eddy wasn't stupid. This wasn't a regular job. "I need time to think about this and get my things in order."

"Fair." Don sighed. "If you want to get this guy, this is the way, Eddy. I got wind of a job that this guy Pete was putting together in Peru. He was seeking additional assistance. I don't do that kind of work anymore, but Pete does a lot. We compared notes and put two and two together."

"I can stall Shawn for a little while longer. Tell him I need to give work notice. He's expecting me to head to Peru soon. Huancayo. Says I'll get the villa address when I get there. An eight-hour drive in the rainy season. It's a trap," Eddy said.

Don chuckled. "Probably is."

Eddy smirked, but the chill down his spine told him the truth. *I'm about to step into something I can't walk away from.*

CHAPTER 17:
BACK TO THE BUMP AND GRIND

Monday, 19 January 2015, 0750 hours
Eddy's house, Grapevine, Texas

Eddy Ludt found himself unable to sleep all night long. He had too many things on his mind. Seventy milligrams of melatonin didn't even do the trick. It was a mixture of excitement and anxiety. He was no operator and not much of a fighter himself.

He was a loner. Shawn's betrayal still burned. Eddy had his scars, both physical and psychological. To this day, he despised bullies and manipulators, which was why he despised Shawn. Shawn was everything Eddy had sworn he would never become: a fake, a fraud, untrue to his word. Any man who does that needs to turn in his "man card." *Have I become this man myself?*

At 0800, Eddy got out of bed. He'd never been one to dilly-dally in bed, and he wasn't usually grumpy when he got up.

He squeezed in some pushups and a quick run. He was starting work at 1000 because Rosa had changed his schedule again. *My God, she hates me!* After a quick hard-boiled egg breakfast with coffee and orange juice, he headed for his prized Mustang 5.0. The clock on his dashboard read 0910 as he pulled out of his garage, his mechanical steed obedient in every way.

The traffic was moderate for the DFW area today. *At least it's still moving. I hate being at a complete stop,* Eddy thought.

Another glance at the dashboard showed 0945 as he pulled into the corporate headquarters parking lot. Some people were outside talking or glued to their phones. To his distaste, Eddy saw Rosa on one of her smoke breaks and wondered how such an annoying person managed to keep from getting canned herself.

Rosa sneered and stared at Eddy, but gave up when he ignored her. She seemed obligated to utter disparaging remarks at Eddy, and today was no exception.

"Late again, are we, Eddy?" she demeaned.

Rosa was dressed in gray slacks and talking to one of her man-hating friends in the smoking area, exchanging stories of how the men in their lives had wronged them.

Eddy forced a smile but narrowed his eyes. "No, actually, you changed my schedule again, so I have about ten minutes to spare, not to mention I can flex fifteen minutes, per company policy."

He was emboldened by the prospect of the new job. *Bitch!*

"Well, I hope you're a little quicker this week. Life is only so long. Good to see you finally learned how to tuck your shirt in." Rosa smirked.

Eddy thought about the upcoming adventure, his army reserve tours, and his hobbies. *Life is too short.*

He looked back and forth between the building that tracked his time with a card reader and his Mustang, then back at the building, and then again at the Mustang. *Fuck this shit,* he thought. *I'm sick and tired of living by everyone else's rules. I'm turning Shawn in and changing my life when I return.*

Eddy marched inside, but instead of going to his cubicle, he went to the HR department.

"Hi, I would like to give twenty-four days' notice to resign from the company. Also, I'm going to cash in my twenty-four days' sick time," Eddy stated politely. "I'm getting pains in my head and my butt from Rosa Lemoria."

He showed his employee badge and gave all the appropriate information. After Eddy filled out the paperwork, including cashing in the sick leave, he handed it to the woman behind the desk and, without waiting for a response, headed to his cubicle, stopping only to grab an empty box he found on the way.

"What are you doing!" Rosa snapped, catching Eddy packing away his belongings.

"You remember when I told you that you didn't know everything? Well, I just quit." Eddy smiled like he was a kid again at his birthday party. "I bet you didn't know that, did you?" *Bitch.*

Rosa stormed to her office, perhaps to make some calls, possibly to confirm that Eddy was telling the truth.

When Eddy passed Rosa's office on his way out, she looked up to see him carrying an overflowing box. "Oh yeah, one other thing. Fuck you, you fucking bitch!" Eddy said triumphantly.

Then he left, being exceptionally polite to everyone before Rosa could recover from the shock. Eddy had never dared to speak to her like that before.

Time to reinvent myself, he thought. *Slay one dragon at a time.*

He tossed the box in the trunk, got behind the wheel of his beloved Mustang, and revved his engine loudly before peeling out.

"Yee haw!" he shouted.

Eddy was a free man at last.

He called Don from the car and put him on speaker. "Let's get this show on the road. I just quit!"

"Way ahead of you. I knew you'd take the job." Don laughed, "You start tomorrow. I'll call my contacts at Silent Wolf and work out the details. You're getting trained by the best that money can buy."

Eddy responded, "You got it. Oh, and pick a different airline, OK? Ultimate Flights sucks, anyway. I'm paying full fare or miles from now on."

CHAPTER 18:
HOUSTON

Tuesday, 20 January 2015, 0600 hours
Eddy's house, Grapevine, Texas

Eddy woke to his alarm, heart pounding before his eyes even opened.

His left hand trembled as he grabbed his phone. He checked the screen with his unsteady hand. Nothing new. _Is that good or bad?_

He rolled out of bed. He'd packed yesterday, leaving just toiletries.

He worked out harder than he had since Basic Training in 1989. Eddy ran hard down the historic Grapevine streets. The cold stung his exposed face. He did pushups, crunches, and squats.

By 0720 hours, he'd finished his exercise regimen but still couldn't shake his nervous energy. Kosovo. Iraq. Afghanistan. Those tours hardened him. But Peru was new.

His phone rang with the James Bond theme song. It was Donald.

"Staff Sergeant Delcey, this is Eddy Ludt, although I'm more commonly known by my code name 530953. I accept this mission and will fulfill it or die trying."

Donald ignored the joke. "OK, Eddy, you fly out on American Airlines from DFW to Houston at 1900 hours. You'll be picked up at the airport, and your two teammates will meet you. Look, you're a great guy, but you're not an operator, OK? Don't get your ass killed trying to be cool. This isn't a training exercise. I trust you, but you're there to learn, so be humble. And take it easy on the alcohol. Just because it's free doesn't mean you have to drink it all.

Yeah, you're right. Lately, instead of a six-pack, I've been looking more like a keg. I worked out today. You would've been proud. But it'll take every bit of those three weeks to start seeing the results.

On his wrist, he wore his trusty Citizen Professional Divers watch, bought in the Bahamas in June 2013. It was suitable for 300 meters. It didn't make him a better diver, but he felt it looked more professional to be diving with one of these. Luminous white dots appeared in place of numbers on the face. *I can't take you to Peru, my friend, but I'll take you to Houston with me.*

"I'm going to need to get in shape."

"Just remember, round is a shape too. See you later. Call me anytime. Wake me up if you need to."

Eddy looked at the list he'd created to make sure all loose ends were taken care of.

- ✓ Call the credit card company. Please let them know that I'll be traveling to Peru in a few weeks and will be charging a lot, so they should not lock my account.

- ✓ Put ten thousand dollars on the credit card. Eddy always felt that would make it more likely his card would be accepted. It probably didn't matter much, but he was a creature of habit. That much money should cover any unexpected emergencies.
- ✓ Purchase travelers' insurance starting from the date of departure and effective for a period of three months. That should be more than enough time.
- ✓ Discover the types of diseases I may encounter in Peru and receive the appropriate medication to prevent them.
- ✓ Pay to have the house professionally cleaned by a maid I trust and leave the money on the counter. A spy should return home to a clean house, after all.
- ✓ Sever ties. A few names were scribbled down, and he'd made a few phone calls, each taking a great burden off Eddy. But the main one was yet to come. Shawn, or whatever his real name was, puppet master of lies and deception.
- ✓ Pray and ask forgiveness for all his sins and any he might commit in the next few weeks.

Yes, I did them all. This was evidenced by the checkmarks Eddy had placed beside each task on the list.

He noted a Shakespearean twist to this situation. He and Shawn were both fakes. Eddy because he misfired and got lucky. Shawn, because the truth was less prevalent than the lies in his life. It saddened Eddy that he had anything in common with someone he loathed.

He recalled Shawn trashing his car after taking it for a joyride, with Eddy jumping on the hood of the Chevy Malibu, trying to stop him. Shawn had driven the car backward and forward in the mud and over rocks, laughing the whole time, left it running with the windshield wipers on, and then conveniently forgot it the next day, like so many other things.

Shawn was Eddy's real dragon to slay. Closure on this fiend who abused women and stole from Eddy and his friends.

Eddy was still wearing his blue Crocs, without socks. He wore a pair of Rip Curl swimming trunks featuring white skeleton heads. He'd bought them on a diving trip to Australia. He also had on a black muscle shirt. He'd be getting dirty in South America tracking down that parasite, and there was no sense in messing up good clothes before the trip.

He texted Shawn to stall for time. Shawn had already been waiting a long time, so it didn't make sense to stall too long. He might find someone else.

Hey Shawn, I think I'm going to take you up on your offer. This is Tuesday. Please give me until Friday to submit my two-week resignation in person to my boss. It's a big step, and he's on vacation until then. Maybe you could send me some information so I could get started on the job now?

Shawn called almost immediately, but Eddy ignored it. He had more control over the situation by texting.

Eddy ordered pizza to be delivered at 1400. He'd been eating up everything in the refrigerator since the day before, and there wasn't much left. Only canned stuff remained. He didn't want to return to a science experiment after Peru, with green things trying to crawl out of the fridge and stink up his place.

He took a long shower, prayed, and considered his next move. Clarity never came easily when Shawn was involved. He'd have to earn it the hard way.

Afterward, he threw on a pair of green swim trunks and a t-shirt he'd bought in Kwajalein Atoll. He sat at his desk with a notepad, thinking about what needed to happen next. His dive watch showed 1344, which meant it was 1244 in Peru. They didn't observe daylight savings.

First, he called Delcey to tell him what was happening and to get some moral support.

About fifteen minutes later, Shawn followed up with a long message. Whenever Shawn got long-winded like this, it meant he was drunk or worse. Being in one of the cocaine capitals of the world, Eddy assumed the latter.

He looked at the screen, took a breath, and read the message. It was obvious Shawn was drunk or, knowing Shawn, high.

Hi Ed, call me bro. I have a fantastic deal for you. You aren't very grateful for all I did for you. You see, it's kind of like in the Bible when that man was not grateful after he was forgiven for a lot, but then he couldn't forgive a little. As for the best man's gift you got so upset about, I never told you I got you for you. You must have me confused with someone else. God tells us not to bear false witness against our neighbors, Eddy. Are you sure you're mentally stable? That intel you got about the roads is bullshit. No problem there.

Yep, he's on something. You're a liar through and through, Shawn. You can't open your mouth without lying.

The sermons Shawn gave on campus funded his tuition, his apartment, and his wild parties with women, who either willingly or unwillingly participated in his sick sexual tastes. *I didn't want to believe it because you were my friend, or so I thought, but a preponderance of the evidence, and later encounters with these women, confirmed it.*

"Brother." Shawn made good money preaching as a side hustle.

Shawn was a negotiator, so Eddy needed to make him feel like he had the upper hand. Pete had told him he needed several weeks of training from Silent Wolf before starting the job, so Eddy used that as leverage. He texted back.

I need three weeks from this coming Friday. If you can't provide that, I won't be able to help you.

Ten minutes later came the angry reply.

You don't need to give your job notice. Eddy! Listen to me! You're fucking quitting. What is wrong with you? Do you not understand what it means to quit? One million dollars! Think! Tax-free! Okay, I suppose I'll have to pass this deal on to someone else.

He's sighing now, Eddy imagined. Same fake exhale like always, trying to act like I'm missing out on the deal of a lifetime.

Shawn hadn't changed. Not even the euphoric high of whatever he was on could override his personality. He would pull someone in, then control them with crumbs of kindness. Stockholm Syndrome.

I'm probably not the first person he called. Either they said no, or they couldn't handle the job. Hell, maybe they tried and failed.

He closed his eyes. Shawn's a gambler. I'm not. I played it safe. It's time to move outside your comfort zone, Eddy. He won't expect a bluff.

Eddy called him.

Shawn answered, already annoyed. "Eddy, what's your problem? Can't you figure out that this is the right thing? Get down here right now!"

Eddy listened to him vent, then struck. "OK, Shawn, thanks for the two hundred thousand dollars for doing nothing. You need me. I don't need you. If you didn't need me, you wouldn't have called. So, let's be civil, you chickenshit motherfucker. I don't fucking work for you anymore."

He hung up. Eddy had never done that before. It wouldn't be a real win unless Shawn called back.

He waited. Then texted Delcey. Don once told him he wasn't the smartest guy on the planet. *But Don doesn't know Shawn.* Shawn thrived on power and control. If Eddy could make him feel he was losing both, he'd come crawling back.

The phone rang. Eddy ignored it.

Then it rang again. And again. It went to voicemail. Eddy listened.

"You, ungrateful narcissist! You blew me off after my wedding, criticizing my church. Read Brené Brown's *Dare to Lead.* Fix your perfectionism!"

I know what you're doing, thought Eddy. Shawn was trying to provoke a reaction, banking on Eddy's inability to resist the money. But Eddy stayed calm. He jotted down everything that happened, the time it happened, and any detail he could remember.

Two full hours passed. He started to believe he'd lost the fish.

Finally, two and a half hours later, the message came.

Eddy, I forgive your treatment of me just as our Lord and Savior forgives you. OK, I'll give you three weeks. I'm not paying you to insult me and abuse me. Make your flight on February 12th to Miami. From there, you will meet with a private pilot contact I have arranged. Please let me know when you arrive in Miami, and I'll provide you with the information.

Eddy sat with it. Can I pull this off? Can I beat Shawn at his own game? I've never been to Peru, and I won't blend in at all—time for some serious research.

He would be part of a small team to keep things quiet. But he'd lean on them heavily.

He decided to wait at least an hour before replying. He used his laptop, linked to his phone, to make sure every word was precise.

OK, this is how this is going to work. When I get to Miami, you will text me the name and the number of that pilot and anything else that I need to know. I'll take another phone with me to Peru, and I'll call you from my Peruvian number. I do not want any of your guys picking me up at the airport either. If I spot them, I'm done. I'll come back. I'm telling a lot of people I'm going to Peru on vacation to see an old friend who moved there. The specifics of what is happening, including your name and the number you called me from, and what you are paying me to do are in an envelope marked "Open 01 April 2024." If I do not return, the police will find my envelope. My mother will open it also, as she is coming by once a day to feed my dog. That's how it's going to be. If you have a problem with that, find someone else.

An hour later, Shawn replied.

Fine, but only on the condition that you let my guy pick you up in Lima. This is not negotiable.

Eddy felt empowered. He wasn't used to standing up for himself to Shawn, and Shawn wasn't used to being spoken to that way.

The time was 1700, and Eddy needed to leave. He knew from experience that arriving an hour early should be fine, but there was no sense in risking it.

He double-checked his bags, passport, money, and other items, and reviewed his list to make sure all his bases were covered. His shots from the army reserves covered him medically for anything he was likely to encounter.

Eddy dressed in blue jeans and packed three pairs of cargo pants. He decided he didn't need any fancy clothes, ties, or jewelry.

He wore a sweatshirt over his white t-shirt, with his leather jacket packed away. He was heading to Miami, where it was warm, and then to Peru, where it was summer, although cold at night in Huancayo.

Eddy called an Uber.

He spoke to his dog, Dina, and gave her a hug. "It's OK, baby, I'll be back, and we'll go somewhere and play for a long time. You be a good girl, OK?

The Uber came, and Eddy stepped out.

Then, Eddy Kevin Ludt, a bullied child who was socially awkward, clumsy, and disorganized, left his house in Grapevine, Texas, to be a dog of war.

Yeah, right.

CHAPTER 19:
THE SOUTH AMERICA ADVENTURE

Tuesday, 20 January 2015, 1643 hours
American Airlines ticket counter, Dallas/Fort Worth
International Airport, Irving, Texas

Eddy reached DFW with time to spare, dragging his suitcase behind him. He had already checked in online, so no worries.

She smiled without looking up.

"Where are you headed today, sir?" Anita asked.

"Nonstop to Houston Bush Airport, flight 809 at 1900, please. Here is my passport, and I have already printed my boarding pass. I have one bag to check here, and I just went through it. Also, I need to check my firearms, please, and they are in this carrying case. I have no ammunition."

Eddy smiled and tried to look confident so the whole thing would go smoothly.

"Yes, Ma'am. Have a good night, Anita."

The road ahead would be anything but easy, and Peru would be the most challenging part of all.

Eddy needed something to calm his nerves. Somewhat to his alarm, he remembered that D.B. Cooper, the criminal who hijacked a flight from Portland to Seattle in 1971, drank bourbon to do the same.

What the hell, he thought.

He got up and approached the bar.

"May I have a double bourbon, neat, please, and also a bottle of water?"

Once at the table, Eddy sipped his drink and checked his email. There was an email from Pete with a number for him to call.

He pulled his phone from his pocket and dialed the number. It rang twice before someone picked up.

"Wise Dog," said the person on the other end.

"Hi," Eddy replied. "This is Eddy Ludt. Pete told me to call this number. Who's this?"

"Wise Dog," came the reply.

"Is this some sort of joke?" Eddy asked.

"Nope, just my name."

Eddy grinned. Although he found it hard to do without laughing, he reluctantly called the man "Wise Dog," just as he had insisted.

"OK, Wise Dog. I worked with the Special Forces in Afghanistan, but I've always been conventional forces myself. You know my flight. I researched the Silent Wolf campus. Sounds like you have quite the training ground there."

Wise Dog answered, "You're going to be fine, Eddy. We're the best of the best at what we do. You're getting private lessons. I'll pick you up personally and give you a tour of the campus tonight until you're too tired or bored to see any more.

"Pete and I don't intend for you to be doing any of the fighting, but we can't control events, and there are many unknowns. You will be trained for the worst-case scenario. We are starting easy. You've had a hectic few days. The following day, you are working out with Pete and me. Pete is an animal, but you are no good if we break you. Your mission is more about finesse than fighting. You'll be fine. Enjoy your food, your drinks, and prepare for an adventure."

Finesse over fighting, Eddy repeated to himself. That's good. I'm not twenty anymore.

Eddy finished his dinner, packed away his laptop, and headed to the gate.

CHAPTER 20:
SILENT WOLF HEADQUARTERS

Tuesday, 20 January 2015, 2100 hours
Houston Hobby International Airport, Houston, Texas.

American Airlines flight 809 arrived at the gate in Houston, Texas, at 2100 hours. Eddy called Wise Dog to let him know he was at baggage claim, then quickly found the office to reclaim his checked firearms.

Waiting for him when he returned were Wise Dog and Peter Zhao. Peter held a gigantic white sign that said, "Hi Eddy, Let's Party! Sunset Cruises." Both men were dressed nicely but not in a flashy way, in polo shirts and slacks.

Eddy extended his hand to Wise Dog. "Eddy, nice to meet you in person."

"Wise Dog," the intimidating man shot back.

Guess he wasn't going to budge on this one. He liked his call sign. Come to think of it, he resembled a pit bull in Eddy's mind.

Pete smiled. "Eddy, I'm Pete, Peter, whatever you want to call me. The bank has given the green light on a significant amount of funding just for you. As my good friend Donald Rumsfeld said, 'We fight with the army we have.'"

"OK, look, Wise Dog told me he would give me a tour of the campus tonight, and I appreciate it, but I think I'd appreciate my sleep more, and my body will thank you if we take this same tour as a brown bag lunch tomorrow," Eddy stated apologetically.

Wise Dog thought about this for a few seconds, then gave a nod of approval. "I like a man who knows what he wants in life. Have it your way. What kind of a pistol do you have?"

"I have a Browning Hi-Power nine-millimeter."

Wise Dog said, "A good, reliable choice."

Eddy's bags were loaded into a silver Ford Expedition SUV. He placed his Pelican case with the three firearms in the back of the SUV.

The driver was younger than the other two Silent Wolf employees. Eddy was given the front passenger seat.

The driver reached over. "William Renfro. Nice to meet you."

Eddy shook the man's hand with a firm grip. "It is nice to meet you also. Eddy Ludt. I've only heard good things about Silent Wolf."

"Don't believe everything you hear," Wise Dog said from the back, directly behind Eddy. "Just kidding, dude. We'll take you right to your hotel. Catch as much sleep as you can. Breakfast starts at 0600, and you need to be there. We'll rendezvous at 0645, so bring your 'go bag[3]' with you. You won't need much. Wear comfortable clothing. Bring a notepad and a pen. We'll give you new tech. We have no way of knowing if your belongings have already been compromised, but please bring them with you, anyway. We'll transfer all the files you need while scanning for malware."

"Yeah, got it," was Eddy's only remark before he dozed off. He slept until they reached the hotel.

Wise Dog, Pete, and Will carried Eddy's stuff and checked him in.

Eddy already had a room paid for at the Lone Star Luxe Hotel, as he would be staying there instead of the campus facilities.

Once upstairs, Wise Dog and Pete moved all of Eddy's things into his room on the fourth floor.

Despite being tired, Eddy took a moment to look around the spacious room. It was rather large, larger than he'd ever stayed in. There was a king-size bed, a full bath with a tub, a large flat-screen TV, a full refrigerator, plus a fully stocked mini fridge and a small kitchen with a gas stove, microwave, utensils, glasses, and silverware. A drip coffee maker and a French press, which Eddy preferred, sat on the counter by the sink.

There was also complimentary food and additional beverages, including both non-alcoholic and alcoholic options.

3   **Go bag:** Military slang for a bag prepared in case a military member needs to leave in a hurry due to an emergency of some sort.

The clock on the wall showed 0030 hours.

"Help yourself to whatever's here," said Wise Dog.

Wise Dog had more experience as an instructor than Pete, so Pete allowed him to take the lead in Eddy's training, even though Pete was technically "senior" to Wise Dog in Silent Wolf.

One thing members of Silent Wolf appreciated was that everything centered on mission success. The most competent individual for a job was placed in charge.

Silent Wolf had their hierarchy, but for their missions, this structure sometimes changed. There was no height and weight test like in the military. There was a regular, mandatory, and tough-as-nails physical fitness test for their operatives before they went into the field.

Members were encouraged to further their education, and Silent Wolf often covered the costs. When a member retired from fieldwork, they could become analysts or pursue other opportunities within the company. There were also employees who only taught specialized training within the mandatory monthly range, including hand-to-hand combat, evasive driving, room clearing, and the like.

"OK," said Wise Dog. "See you at 0600. Do not be late, Eddy. We're treating you with big-boy rules as we believe you to be a professional. But get your ass up early enough."

Eddy nodded. "Thanks," he said. "I'll be there at 0600."

Wise Dog extended his hand. "We are going to customize your Browning and put a laser sight on it. I want to take it from you now so that our armorer can have that done by the time you start training tomorrow. He gets up early, just like us."

Eddy was embarrassed. *Do I even have a choice?* "Ok, sure," he replied.

He opened the gun case, pulled out the Browning, checked it to ensure it was not loaded, and then placed it back inside, along with the two dial locks.

Peter smiled and extended his hand. "You got this, Eddy."

Eddy just nodded this time but said nothing to either.

When they left, he immediately called Delcey.

The phone rang three times before Don Delcey picked up. While it was ringing, Eddy turned out the light because he could feel a headache coming on. He lay on his bed.

"Haaloo Eddy, is that you?" Donald Delcey yawned into his receiver.

Eddy held his cell phone in his right hand and covered his face with his left, pushing off first his left sneaker with his right foot and then his right. "Yeah, I'm sorry to call you like this, but you told me I could, and they're taking my cell phone away from me tomorrow. I'm scared, man. What have you gotten me into here? You didn't tell me everything. I'm not sure if I can call you after that. The hotel has a landline, but who knows, man?"

"Relax, Ed, these guys are there to help you. They are not going to break you down first like they do in military training. You are already in the military. They'll transfer the phone numbers, but they don't know if your phone has been tampered with. Don't be surprised if they give you some new clothes also." Don was slowly coming awake as he spoke with Eddy. "Dude, it may not be the same cell phone, but I bet you will have all the same information."

Don's voice had a soothing effect on Eddy, and he was calming down. *I can't believe these guys do this stuff all the time.*

"Eddy," Don continued, "go to sleep now. Get up when they tell you and do whatever they tell you to do. You're smart. Sometimes, you don't give yourself enough credit. Shawn won't be counting on you having the training that they are going to give you. It will surprise him."

"I guess you're right, Don. Sorry to wake you up when you're trying to get some shut-eye." He felt a little silly for jumping to conclusions.

"Don't apologize, just calm down. Call whenever you need to. If I don't pick up right away, I'll pick up when I can." Don seemed exceptionally understanding.

"I'll talk to you later, Don. Thanks," Eddy replied.

"Later, Ed."

Eddy ended the call.

He quickly unpacked his hygiene kit and the vitamins that he took daily. He found the melatonin and took 30 milligrams, hoping it would do the trick without rendering him too tired in the morning.

Oh well, it's my first day. They would have to understand.

Eddy said a long prayer before he went to sleep.

CHAPTER 21:
A GENTLEMAN'S COURSE
IN KILLING

Wednesday, 21 January 2015, 0500 hours
Eddy's hotel room, Houston, Texas

Eddy woke up and went through his morning ritual. He played bullet chess on his iPad against whoever chess.com matched him with, checked social media, then headed to the bathroom to start preparing for the day.

He dressed quickly, putting on brown cargo pants, white socks, Reebok running shoes, and a long-sleeve shirt from a dive trip. It showed a skeleton pirate on a ship holding a lantern with the caption, "Prepare to be boarded." He added a black belt.

At 0547, Eddy left his room, closed the door, and headed to the elevator. He found the breakfast area on the ground floor. The young girl at the reception desk smiled pleasantly at him, and he nodded back.

Eddy smiled mid-yawn. "Good morning," he said, forcing cheer into his voice.

He saw the two sliding doors at the entrance open to the same three men in black polo shirts and cargo pants who had met him at the airport the previous day.

All three carried what looked like electronic tablets with styluses attached.

Wise Dog spoke up first. "Alright, brother! We didn't have to get you. You came to us. Grab some chow. Stay away from the complimentary champagne, though. Save that for Saturday night."

Pete added, "We're headed over there ourselves. You get enough sleep, man?"

"Yeah, I think I'm good," replied Eddy.

Eddy saw the omelets and decided to have one. They were harder to make than hard-boiled, soft-boiled, or fried eggs, so he rarely made them himself. His cooking skills were more suited to barbecue, spaghetti, hot dogs, and sandwiches.

He stood in the short line, and after two minutes, it was his turn. "I would like two omelets, please, with egg whites, cheese, onion, tomato, green pepper, and bacon."

The chef nodded, and Eddy was surprised by how quickly his meal was ready. The chef prepared his order just the way that he asked and the omelet looked splendid!

He took his tray to the buffet area and grabbed fruit, cereal, and orange juice.

Wise Dog, Pete, and Will sat in a booth. Wise Dog and Pete were on one side, while Will, with all his freckles and a scar on his chin, was on the other. He scooted over when Eddy appeared next to him.

This time, Pete spoke first. "OK, like I said last night, we're all professionals here. Will is new, too, but we treat him with respect. He was once part of the security detail for the U.S. Ambassador with another company at the Embassy in Baghdad, Iraq. We offered him better money and better hours, plus living in the United States most of the time, and there you have it, we got him."

Eddy sighed. "How much time do we have before we need to leave and head into work?" he asked. "What kind of training am I in for? Military Police get much more extensive training with pistols than normal soldiers, but I have a feeling this is on a whole different level. Do I have to sign a waiver or anything?"

Will answered. "It's 0630. Training starts at 0800. It's only about a fifteen-minute drive from here. So, please try to finish up within the next ten minutes or so, okay? We need to process you before training. Tomorrow, we'll come earlier to work out before breakfast and give ourselves more time. We wanted you to get some sleep last night, so we didn't do it today."

The four finished up their breakfasts, mostly in silence, knowing time was of the essence.

Eddy grabbed his backpack, with his jacket tied to it, and his laptop bag, and followed them.

Will walked quickly and opened the doors for the others. Eddy placed his black backpack and laptop bag, which held his PC and iPad, in the back of the SUV.

The time was 0648. Will started the car and pulled out of the parking space.

Wise Dog sat next to Eddy and settled on some hip-hop music. He lay back and took a nap while Pete spoke a little to Will and adjusted the radio.

Eddy glanced at the street behind them. A black SUV sat idling half a block away, its windows tinted, engine humming low. The rear passenger window rolled down halfway, and Eddy saw a man holding something to his face.

Possibly a phone?

The SUV was there only a few seconds before pulling away into traffic.

I've always been the paranoid type.

$$\text{\$\$\$\$\$\$}$$

Silent Wolf's campus appeared large to Eddy, with several layers of fencing and a lot of shade from trees and canopies to hide what the fences contained from snooping eyes.

The standard rent-a-cop, dressed in a blue uniform and armed with a Glock in a holster, stood guard, likely not allowed onto the campus. He was the first level of security before they were thoroughly searched. This was where they parked.

The facility reminded Eddy of many military ones he'd seen, where the less-trained guards formed the outer ring. They caught honest people who were confused and those who were curious. The guards at the next level would be more highly trained and better paid.

Will spoke up. "OK, Eddy, the movie is over for now. Time to make your own action."

"Hand over your military ID or driver's license, please," the tall guard politely asked Eddy.

Eddy handed him his driver's license nervously, wondering what he was getting himself into. *First my pistol, and now my driver's license?*

"You will get it back when you leave, sir. They take security seriously here. Once you have a Silent Wolf ID today, they won't keep it next time you come. At the second security gate, they'll keep your other ID. Same drill, more security." The guard smiled and stepped into his shack.

Will pulled a placard from between the seats that showed the Silent Wolf emblem of a black wolf with yellow eyes, lean and stalking its prey in the night, with a full moon above it to the right.

"Good morning, Orlando," Will said as he handed him all four identifications.

Will knew the drill, so he popped the hood and the back of the vehicle before anyone said anything.

"Good morning, Will. I see we have a guest this morning."

Orlando walked around the vehicle with a mirror mounted on the end of a long pole that allowed him to inspect underneath. He examined all areas of the vehicle. It reminded Eddy of the vehicle searches he'd performed and been subject to in Kosovo, Iraq, and Afghanistan.

Pete said, "This is where we all get to sit under the shade and drink water while they check our vehicle. Leave the doors open. Will, please pop the gas tank. Come with me, Eddy."

Eddy saw the clock on the dashboard read 0705 when all four men stepped out.

While the guard with a German shepherd checked the engine, the trunk, the glove box, and all other crevices inside the vehicle, Pete walked around the corner of a fifteen-foot-high barrier wall. There were comfortable chairs and cold-water bottles available. Eddy grabbed one and broke the seal.

Once the guard and the dog were satisfied with the search, he motioned for the four men to return.

Orlando looked at the passengers and lingered slightly on Eddy as they resumed their seats.

He pulled out a laminated card with letters and numbers on it from the guard shack and handed it to Eddy. "You will get your driver's license back when you return this. Welcome to Silent Wolf, Mr. Ludt. Enjoy your time on our campus."

Will drove into the lot and parked in a space that matched the placard on the windshield.

Eddy saw that the campus was enormous inside as well. Almost everything was hidden behind walls, but he could already hear a lot of shooting and laughing. People were running drills, engaging in physical training, and practicing close-quarters combat. It looked like a campground.

Pete explained, "Eddy, here we have classrooms to rival any university, and professors are brought in to teach. Money talks, and we spend a lot of it."

Signs read: "No photography for *any* reason" and "Leave your cellular phones inside Checkpoint 2, along with any other electronics."

Multiple cameras monitored the parking lot, and guards patrolled periodically. He spotted another Belgian Shepherd sniffing vehicles.

I feel like I'm being sent to prison.

Pete said, "OK, inside, they will take your cell phone and electronics. They are expecting you. The contents will be scanned for viruses, worms, and other malicious threats. Then they'll be transferred, minus any malware or pornography, to another PC, iPad, or iPhone. You'll use these with a new number. Don't stress. This is normal.

"You'll be given fake identification only for emergencies. Obviously, it's illegal to use fake IDs, so only do that if you absolutely must. Otherwise, use the real stuff. You can stay for ninety days as a U.S. citizen without a visa, so don't take unnecessary risks. You've got time to complete your mission. More inside. Let's go."

Pete led the way, Wise Dog followed, and Eddy came next. Will trailed after them, having secured the vehicle.

They walked to a single entrance guarded by a huge man, likely of Samoan or Tongan descent. He had a barrel chest and a short beard.

Pete showed his ID, and the other three wore their Silent Wolf badges.

"Hey, Tony. He's getting his ID today. Show him your military ID, Ed."

Eddy complied, and the guard saw all four identifications.

Probably nothing, Eddy thought, but after years of working in intelligence, that familiar itch between his shoulder blades never completely went away.

"OK, have a good day," the guard said.

This reminded Eddy of a sitcom where a secret agent had to pass through twelve layers of clearance to get to his desk. Only this wasn't a comedy.

CHAPTER 22:
LET THE GAMES BEGIN

Wednesday, 21 January 2015, 0715 hours
Silent Wolf headquarters, Houston, Texas

Wise Dog gave Eddy the initial rundown. "Silent Wolf is a high-security facility with multiple clearance levels, each granting access based on role and necessity. Information is tightly controlled. Clearance dictates access.

"There is a color system to indicate the level of access a person has inside the Silent Wolf compound. A red badge is for someone, such as yourself, who someone with appropriate clearance must accompany. A yellow badge is what most people wear. It entitles them to most areas in the compound but not to locations with the most sensitive information. Green badges grant freedom to roam wherever they want. There are numbers and letters on badges for more sensitive areas, but you don't have to worry about that now."

A conveyor belt and bag scanner was in place as another security check, like what Eddy had encountered at airports, with someone studying the contents from a computer monitor. There was also a metal detector with a guard on the other side.

Before reaching the detector, a retinal scanner was first encountered, featuring red and green indicator lights. Below it was another scanner for the color-coded employee badge. Each employee had to scan their badge and then their retina to verify the match.

In Eddy's case, he wasn't an employee. He had to fill out paperwork, turn over two forms of identification, and wear a laminated red badge with a white band at the top.

The guard wrote with a dry-erase black marker: "Edward Kevin Ludt," along with the last four digits of Eddy's social security number, then took a photo of him wearing the badge.

Eddy stepped up to the scanner. It, of course, flashed red. The guard typed into a keypad to link the data to Eddy's photo, then instructed him to place the contents of his pockets into a storage container and power off all electronics. Eddy complied without hesitation.

The other three members of the group remained quiet while the guards performed the inspection.

Pete finally spoke. "OK, Eddy, we need to take you to see the big man first. I can't use his facilities without prior approval. I only told him what I had to. He's receiving compensation for letting us use his facilities, but this is a handshake deal I brokered between Marcus, my Uncle Tommy, and myself. He just wants to meet you. He's fine with us taking on some side jobs, as long as he's informed about them. Marcus hates to get blindsided, but he doesn't mind us using his facilities, ranges, or anything else as long as we pay for it. He keeps us happy, and we keep working for him."

Alright, whatever, dude. There are so many layers here, I'm expecting to meet M.

The four moved through the rest of security without incident.

They reached a set of electric golf carts. Will climbed into one and said, "I get to drive this, too. Hop in, your chariot awaits."

Pete sat next to Will. Wise Dog took the seat behind the driver, and Eddy grabbed the only spot left.

Wise Dog handed him a set of headphones. "Trust me, you'll need these."

It was as if Will had received a mission briefing. He took off, navigating the compound like he'd done it a hundred times.

Pete spoke after about fifteen seconds of silence. "Well, the areas we must go through first are the gun ranges, every type of small arms range you can imagine. We charge a lot for our services, but we're the best there is."

The campus consisted of nearly identical buildings, each distinguished only by the type of training conducted inside. Many served as firearms ranges, with specific calibers posted near the entrances and along the exterior walls.

Pete explained that the shooting areas on all the ranges were below ground for added safety. Once inside, people had to descend a level to access the firing lines.

All the ranges were connected underground via secure walkways, allowing for movement between them without stepping outside.

The buildings above ground served mainly as visual markers to help people on carts navigate. It saved time. On the ground floors, classrooms hosted firearm training and video playback sessions showing performance footage from the ranges. Some buildings had multiple floors for expanded instruction.

The cart stopped in front of a tan building with big blue letters over the door:

> *The Guy to Blame for All of This. But*
> *the Buck Doesn't Stop Here.*

Wise Dog smirked. "Our boss has quite a sense of humor."

Eddy had heard of him, Marcus Snooten. He'd been a sniper in the 25th Infantry Division and later the 2nd Ranger Battalion. After ten years in the Army, he earned his degree while still serving, left the military, and worked as a private bodyguard and bounty hunter, also earning his master's degree from Florida State University.

A short stint as a deputy sheriff hadn't been enough for him, so he pivoted to contracting work in Iraq. Marcus realized he could earn more and enjoy it more with his own company. He dumped his savings into a startup that bore the same name he'd earned as a sniper in Bosnia, Iraq, and Afghanistan: Silent Wolf.

Pete picked up the cart radio. "Marcus, this is Pete. We got the intel weenie here in the flesh."

Marcus responded, "What are you waiting for? Bring him in here!"

They arrived at the building. Pete typed a code into the keypad by the door. It beeped and unlocked. The door appeared to be sturdy enough to withstand a direct artillery strike and remain intact.

The walls were reinforced concrete lined with thick interior metal panels. The floor was just as solid, bare concrete beneath worn carpeting.

A large man was talking to a smaller one seated beside him. The clock read 0725. From his stance at the door, and based on news coverage, Eddy recognized Marcus Snooten. The man had occasionally made headlines due to Silent Wolf's controversial contracts.

There had been a serious shootout in Iraq years earlier, with Silent Wolf accused of being a little too eager on the trigger. Marcus was forty-one, lean, and kept his hair close-cropped. Gray flecks showed on the sides of his otherwise reddish-blond hair.

The man seated next to him was stockier, with long, red hair and a face that fit a Viking flick. Both wore long-sleeved shirts with the Silent Wolf emblem and well-worn dark jeans.

"Oh, look, I have a hard-on. What is your wife doing for the next hour?" said the red-haired man.

"Nothing with that little pecker," Marcus shot back.

Wise Dog cleared his throat. "Gentlemen, let's keep this PG. We have some sensitive ears here." He gestured toward Eddy.

Marcus stood up fast. For a smaller guy, he moved with energy.

Eddy noticed freckles across his face as Marcus pumped his hand like a politician. "I'm Marcus. A pleasure to meet you, Eddy. I like to meet the people who'll be using the facility. No issues, buddy. Don't mind Davis, he's the Neanderthal of our little tribe." He gestured with his thumb toward the red-haired man. "We keep him away from the general population, for their safety and his."

Eddy offered the only reply he could think of. "Thank you for letting me use your facility."

Marcus grinned. "OK, get his ass to Winston. I'm a sniper myself, and I think the good Lieutenant Colonel here might've had a stroke of luck in Afghanistan in 2010. I could never have made that shot. With a pistol? Forget it." He winked at Eddy and nodded as if to say, "*It's going to be alright. Your secret's safe with me.*"

Wise Dog glanced at his watch. "It's 0729 hours, and we need to get his ass over to the range. I'll grab some coffees, water, soda, energy drinks, and snacks from the cafeteria. We can't be hurting Winston's feelings like that."

Pete added, "As long as he gets paid, his feelings will be fine. More money for him to buy beers at the VFW[4] and lie about his escapades in Vietnam."

Will grinned. "Let's go, guys. Have fun out there. Let me know if you need anything."

---

4   **VFW:** Stands for Veterans of Foreign Wars. In this instance, the reference is to a VFW bar, where servicemembers who served in the U.S. military during a time of combat operations and their families can enjoy discounted liquor and some food.

CHAPTER 23:
CLASSROOM TIME

Wednesday, 22 January 2015, 0756 hours
Silent Wolf's small arms training facility, Houston,
Texas

Winston, like most military professionals from his era, abhorred starting late. So, he regularly started early, if he could, with plenty of swearing, coffee, and cigarettes. "Work to standard, not to time," is what they had always told him in the Marine Corps, which meant work until your boss tells you that you're done.

To Winston's delight, Eddy knew quite a bit about his pistol. *Maybe there is hope for this geek,* he thought.

Some of the information was useful, but some of it was only good for trying to impress a girl in a bar on Friday night. If nothing else, Winston wouldn't have to treat Eddy like some of the other folks who came here with only limited firearm exposure while in the military. Eddy had some practical knowledge.

In just thirty minutes, they were ready to move to the next phase, called "dry firing," which simply meant going through all the motions of shooting without using ammunition. This was the 21st century; they would incorporate technology. Winston placed a plastic insert where the firing pin would strike the pistol to prevent damage that might come from dry firing. He also attached a laser pointer to the barrel to show where rounds struck on an electronic screen.

At 1143 hours, Winston felt a vibration in his pocket and retrieved his cell phone.

"OK, Eddy. Wise Dog just shot me a chat. He's bringing in some steak and lobster for lunch. He said he wants to check in on you, being the first day and all. We are not going to starve you here, that's for sure. Make sure to stay hydrated and caffeinated. You're doing good. You may be alright after all."

Winston introduced Eddy to the Glock 43. Winston placed the Glock 43 in Eddy's hand. The compact pistol disappeared into his palm, its weight lighter than he expected.

"Perfect for keeping out of sight," Winston said, tapping the slim frame.

Eddy turned it over, frowning at the unfamiliar grip. He aimed it toward the corner, squeezed the trigger once on an empty chamber, then repeated the motion. The awkwardness faded after a few tries, his wrist steadying, his stance loosening. By the time Winston nodded in approval, Eddy's fingers rested on the weapon like they belonged there.

They completed the dry fire training before noon. Eddy was a fast learner. Winston examined the firearms and made some notes in his notebook.

He took out gun oil and carefully lubed the firearms. After a moment, he stopped. "Hey, Eddy, you need to be able to clean your pistols, too. Work on these while I go through the next slides. I'll give you some pointers when you're done."

Eddy looked at the firearms the way some people admire their sports car.

Winston said, "Take a fifteen-minute break, use the head, whatever, and be back at 1215 hours to start these videos on Peru that Wise Dog sent me. They hired a Spanish teacher from some university to come here and give you private lessons after you eat."

Eddy gulped down a whole can of Monster and did a few push-ups before rushing to the restroom.

When he returned, he closed his eyes and stretched out on the floor. Eddy was already feeling the stress. He was a pencil pusher, and he knew it. It didn't matter what kind of car he drove or what guns he owned.

The break was over, and Eddy sat in a comfortable chair with a cup holder. He was reminded of those fancy cinemas where they served food.

The movie started, and Eddy watched videos of Peru while continuing to clean his firearms. Winston noted that although Eddy was sloppy in his appearance, he took great care with his firearms.

Wise Dog walked in with someone who was also wearing a red badge like Eddy. The man was Hispanic, well-groomed, and slender, with his hair pulled back into a ponytail. He carried what appeared to be a picnic basket.

The man removed a cloth covering the basket, and everyone could see some large green fuzzy dice and board games on top. It contained pens, pencils, markers, and other supplies. It looked like someone who had just shown up for the old children's show *Sesame Street*.

"Everyone, I would like you to meet Pedro Leandro. He is originally from Peru. He has a master's degree in Spanish from the University of Madrid, so he is up to task."

Pedro approached Eddy. "Nice to meet you."

"Thank you, sir. It is nice to meet you, too," Eddy replied.

Pedro's eyes widened at the sight of the firearms, and he stepped back. He seemed nervous. Pedro wasn't someone accustomed to seeing weapons. It didn't matter. For what they needed him to do, he didn't have to be.

Wise Dog shot Eddy a look of fear and demand. It was a definite *watch what you say* look.

Wise Dog said, "OK, Eddy, put the pistols over on the table. You can finish cleaning them later. Also, around Pedro, we're only going to talk about Peru and Spanish, everyone. Pete will not be joining us today. He's doing some research on our trip. So, I have lunch here, and we'll enjoy it before Pedro talks us through the culture of Peru. He sent me his own set of slides and movies. Eddy, you're going to get a crash course in Spanish. You can't hope for fluency, but at least you should be able to get by. Pedro, Eddy won't have time to study outside of your class. Make sure he pays attention to you. Every moment counts. Six days per week, classes every day."

"Hey, look, man, with what you're paying me, I'll make it happen, OK?" Pedro set down the small backpack and pulled out basic teaching items: a laser pointer, a pencil case, a notebook, several books, and a few posters.

"Is it OK if I stick some of these up on the walls?" he asked.

"Go for it, and leave them up, buddy. We have this firing range all to ourselves for the next three weeks," Winston said pleasantly. "So, let's make the most of this time while we have it."

Winston was a moody man and prone to profanity. He fit in well here. However, he was a pleasant man when he wanted to be.

"I'm going to go take an extended smoke break while you gentlemen eat. I don't need to know Spanish, nor am I planning a trip to Peru anytime soon." When Winston got back from Vietnam the second time, he kissed the ground and swore he would never leave the United States again, and he'd kept his word so far. He had everything that he needed right here. He didn't lose anything in Vietnam or in any other foreign country. He didn't fight for this country to spend retirement playing global hide-and-seek.

He looked briefly at the posters. They were all handwritten and bore marks of age. It was apparent that Pedro had used these before.

Winston could see Pedro out of the corner of his eye, setting up things on the table to assist him with his classes. He wondered just what Pedro thought of teaching on a shooting range around a bunch of contractors for hire.

It was true that all those people looked the same to Winston. He'd just had an isolated life, mainly associating with people from Texas, outside of his tours in Vietnam.

He walked outside to a covered area with a clear sign indicating that it was a smoking area and joined others sitting out there with blue jeans, baseball caps, and cans of chewing tobacco.

Things continued this way for three weeks. Pete and Wise Dog gave Eddy hand to hand combat training focused on defense instead of offense as his role in this operation was to create an opportunity for Pete and Wise Dog to take Shawn alive while recovering the cryptocurrency key. Ready or not, Eddy was headed to Peru.

He picked up on the marksmanship skills quickly, but the hand-to-hand combat was a different story. Eddy was never coordinated when it came to sports. He could run, swim, and shoot well, but he struggled with sports that required coordination.

He had studied Spanish for four years in high school, and two and a half years in college, so he knew it well enough to order things and get basic directions.

Pete called a meeting immediately after breakfast on Tuesday, the 11th of February, at 0900. He wanted to give Eddy time to eat well, drink plenty of coffee, and feel refreshed.

He pointed to an SUV outside, and they all headed there, checking cell phones and sending messages until they got inside. Then Pete made them put their electronics in a case designed to prevent listening.

Pete said, "Alright, you motherfuckers. This is the plan. Only Wise Dog and I knew about this until now. I didn't even tell my favorite uncle." Few people understood Operational Security. One couldn't reveal a secret if one didn't know it.

Wise Dog rolled his eyes as if he was used to these theatrics.

Pete looked at him. "Don't roll your eyes at me, Clarence, or I'll tear up your Star Trek figures."

Eddy laughed, looking at Wise Dog. "Is that your real name? Clarence? Clarence, what?"

Pete replied, "Clarence Thibodeaux Cooleridge. Also, he's a die-hard Trekkie."

Eddy laughed again, and he understood why Wise Dog went by his call sign instead of his real name. *I would never have figured him for a Trekkie.*

Wise Dog blushed but said nothing.

Eddy had earned the right to a little playful banter.

Pete continued. "Anyway, Shawn has some really good fighters with him. Fortunately for you, they're not good enough because you have us. You're going in the way Shawn told you to. Wise Dog and I are taking commercial airlines. This also means the only weapons we are bringing are multitools. But that's OK. We will acquire weapons.

"From what I've read and heard about this Shawn guy, or whatever the fuck his name is, he'll be underestimating you because he's an arrogant prick. Although the people who are with him know how to fight, I don't think he's much of a fighter. He would rather bullshit his way out than fight."

Now, Wise Dog said, "Apparently, the name he is going by now is the same one you know him by, Shawn Larson. That could mean there's someone else down there in Peru who knew him by the same name, or maybe he just didn't want to have to explain to you why he was going by another name."

Eddy nodded. "He is very smart and knows I would question why he's not using his 'real' name."

Wise Dog continued, "OK, well, you at least knew the guy, kind of, at some point. Nobody else on this operation ever did. Our cover, meaning Pete and I, is adventure tourists taking a few weeks off to appreciate some of the things most American tourists never see. Not all of this is bullshit. I intend to hike some mountains when I get there to acclimate myself. I'll visit all the churches, including the fine Reverend Shawn's, if he attends. His modus operandi is using Christianity to cloak his real intentions."

"We can't let a lot of people in on this, or we would be there already," Pete said. "You told me Shawn set up a driver for you. Don't use him. We've hired our own driver. Shawn will be pissed, but say you know this guy from the Army and he's living in Peru now. His name is Martin Rivadeneira, and this is his fake bio."

Pete handed Eddy some papers. "Don't keep this. Learn it and shred it. It's not a secret, but we can't risk anyone finding out about it. Just keep his contact information in your phone. He speaks English well."

"I'm supposed to call the other driver when I arrive," Eddy said.

Pete shook his head. "Yeah, you told us. Look, call our driver, Martin, and then call the other driver and apologize. I'm sure Shawn already paid him, so he will probably be happy. There is an Airbnb located in the Miraflores district of Lima. We've rented a room for you there for one month. You can keep the firearms there if you decide it is too risky to carry them. The driver will keep his mouth shut, drop you off, and then conveniently turn off his cell phone for the next few weeks.

"We're giving you a debit card with five thousand dollars on it. This is for purchasing things that you do not want Shawn to know about. You may encounter some challenging situations, so stay vigilant.

"You told us your flight goes from Dallas Fort Worth, Texas, to Miami at 0800, just like Shawn wanted. Take these three burner phones. Use the one to communicate with us until you meet your contact in Miami for your southern adventure. Once you meet your contact, use the restroom and destroy the chip inside, just in case. Use another phone once you are safely in Martin's car.

"Call me on it and let me know you are OK. Use these two as much as you like. Keep the last phone in the compartment in your laptop case. I'm giving you a powerful sedative to put in their drinks. This will knock them out for several hours, more than enough time. Use the zip ties just like we showed you. Hands behind the back. Tie the legs too. Something over their mouths in case they wake up. We'll figure out how to spin this to the authorities once we have him back in the States.

"Now, fill out this paperwork to become a licensed security officer with us. If we run into a situation that is difficult to explain regarding your actions in Peru, we'll use this as a cover. I'll make sure you are sworn in. By the time we catch that bastard, my uncle will need to have completely notified and cooperated with the authorities about the money stolen from his bank. The cryptocurrency key is an internal problem that we will handle internally. We'll make sure this operation has legal protections, but we want to have things under control to avoid any embarrassing situations for Trufunds."

Eddy had visions of being hauled off to a jail in Peru, but said nothing.

Wise Dog said, "Today, rest as much as you can, until your driver, Billy Batista, knocks on your door at 1300. You can pack once he arrives.

"A U.S. Marshal connection of ours will meet you at a gas station when Batista stops for gas. He'll talk to you for a while, swear you in as a deputy, and ensure that the proper paperwork is filled out. Pete and I will be sworn in today in a similar manner.

"The trip should be less than four hours. Get on the road by 1400, and even with restroom breaks, you'll be there before 1900. The U.S. Marshal stays in the car and gets dropped off at his aunt's house. Hydrate, meditate, pray, whatever. Remember, Shawn is not expecting you to be prepared.

"We'll get someone to drive you back to Grapevine so you can spend the last night in your own home and, of course, with your dog. You'll be in an SUV, so sit in the back and relax. If you need a drink or two to calm down, I suggest you do it, but no drunkenness. We need you lucid."

At 1300 hours, Eddy awoke to a light knocking on his door.

He opened it just enough to confirm that it was Billy. "Hi, Billy?"

The man who looked back at him had dark blond hair and appeared to be in his thirties. He was about Eddy's height and wore slacks, a light blue polo shirt, and sneakers.

"That's right, my man. I'll be downstairs while you pack up your things. Try to complete it all in about forty-five minutes or so. I want to get on the road close to 1400 hours so we don't get caught up in rush hour traffic."

Eddy tried to smile but failed. "OK, it won't take long."

Without saying another word, Billy headed to the elevator.

Eddy decided against coffee because he was going to try to sleep. However, he would stretch out a bit. He was sore from all the training and wired with nerves about the mission. He needed to be relaxed, and tonight he would focus on sleep.

The phone rang. It's Michael. I mean, Shawn! He can't find out I know his other aliases!

Eddy decided not to answer. Better to check the voicemail and print it to text.

He called Pete immediately on the burner to tell him that he was leaving. He got Pete's voicemail.

That's right. Pete said he was leaving. He's probably already on a flight.

Eddy packed quickly but carefully. He looked at himself in the mirror—*time to slay the dragon.* The most manipulative person he had ever met, and he always got away with it. *Until now,* Eddy thought. *It's judgment day.*

The suitcase thumped against each step as Eddy dragged it down the stairwell. At the door, Billy was already waiting, keys dangling from his hand.

"Morning," Billy said, grabbing the handle and heaving the bag into the back of the SUV.

"Appreciate it," Eddy replied, brushing his palms together.

The two shared a quick smile, nothing more, before Billy slammed the hatch shut. Moments later, the engine rumbled to life, and the tires carried them away from the curb.

Billy had the paperwork ready for the bondsman.

They picked up the bondsman at a gas station after about two hours, and Eddy explained he'd already read the paperwork. The bondsman produced a pen, and Eddy signed.

The remainder of the trip was uneventful, and they took Eddy to his home in Grapevine, Texas.

Dina was tied up to her doghouse in the yard. She barked and wagged her tail when Eddy stepped out of the car.

The marshal helped him with his bags, and Eddy shook hands with Billy and the marshal before they left.

Eddy looked at Dina. "Well, no time like the present, girl." He brought her inside and spent about an hour playing with her. He noticed they did a good job on his house; it was spotless. He liked that. At 1954 hours, he kissed Dina on the forehead and got ready for bed. His flight was at 0800, and he set a wakeup call for 0400.

A phone call came in. It was Shawn. Eddy knew he had to answer this time. He couldn't always be unavailable. That would look too suspicious.

Eddy answered, "Yeah, Shawn, what's up?"

"I was just making sure that you were going to keep your word and not leave me hanging out to dry," Shawn said.

Like you do with everyone else, Eddy thought.

141

"Yeah, of course. I'm flying American to Miami," he replied. He'd booked a first-class ticket and doubted Shawn would complain, considering how much money was on the table.

"OK, well, don't miss it."

Eddy stared at the screen, jaw tight. I'm coming home with you in chains, you bastard. Let's see you smooth-talk your way out of that.

CHAPTER 24:
SANCTIFIED LIES

Shawn and the other two pugilists had hired a local man to drive them to the town of Huancayo, where they would stay overnight in Miraflores. They had too much gear to take a bus, and with no precise return date, they decided to hire someone local who'd take the money and not ask questions. In Huancayo, Shawn was renting a repurposed church building.

He examined the crowds in his new town. He saw them all as lesser. Hispanics and Blacks didn't matter. In his mind, he was the apex.

He stood out in Huancayo, a historic city. It took them nine hours to drive in, factoring in a break for his crew, dinner with their driver, and two restroom stops.

There were better places to hide, such as the jungle, or *selva*, as it was called here, but his crew was small and had a limited footprint. He feared the jungle's larger predators, both human and otherwise. The criminals out there might outgun him.

The people in Huancayo resembled a blend of South American Latinos and Japanese. They were noticeably shorter than the Americans Shawn was used to. He didn't find the local women appealing. They lacked the exotic allure of the Colombians and Venezuelans he had once entertained. To him, they were plain. A man used to venison might've called them gamey. But Shawn, still using the name Shawn Larson, had needs. Like a mechanic, he took whatever parts were available to make something work.

Since leaving sea-level Lima, he had suffered from altitude sickness that wouldn't go away. A dull pain settled in the back of his head, refusing to let up. The colder weather didn't bother him. The roads and buildings were poorly maintained, but the anonymity was worth it. In Lima, he couldn't have disappeared like this.

To blend in better, Shawn began growing a beard and dyed his hair a lighter blond. Still, he stuck out. For this reason, he used his most practiced scam, posing as a representative of Luz del Redentor Internacional.

Shawn knew Trufunds would eventually catch on, so he reached out to former mercenaries who had worked for him before. He needed more muscle for his next heist. The money he'd stolen from Trufunds would help fund it, but he only had access to half of it until that idiot Eddy arrived with the rest.

Huancayo was full of history, like many parts of Peru, but Shawn had no genuine interest in it. He feigned enthusiasm because locals expected it. He needed an excuse to walk around without drawing suspicion. In this town, he could go an entire day without seeing a single gringo.

Shawn had rented a church by making generous donations to local religious and government officials. He even looked the part of a missionary. Inside his office, Amy Grant's *Lamb of God* played softly in the background. The locals were watching him closely.

Shawn's strategy for winning trust was always the same. He bribed those who could be bribed. Those with too much integrity, he threatened. Most eventually found a way to compromise.

They chose this church because it had dozens of places to stash weapons, gold, and other contraband. Their final hotel stay had been paid for using Anna Maria's credit card.

The church's exterior was a white and rusty orange, the tallest building within a five-mile radius. It was about fifty feet high, obviously very old from the cracks seen in the thick walls. From the bell towers, Shawn's crew could observe everything through binoculars and guard their perimeter with rifles.

His first service was scheduled for Sunday. Instead of asking for donations, he handed out 100-sol notes. Some parishioners were disappointed by the practice.

Good riddance. He only wanted people he could manipulate. There were always a few with pesky scruples, people who couldn't be bought.

Shawn had a few girlfriends within three weeks of his arrival. In reality, they were just women he had sex with because he was doing things for them. He was establishing his roots in the community while planning another job. Although the last job was supposed to be his final one, Shawn could never get enough. It was his addiction, the need to always have more.

Monica, a pretty local college student, walked out of the office Shawn had converted into his personal bedroom, buttoning up her shirt. She worked at a nearby store and needed money to make ends meet. Shawn, being a charitable soul, had arranged with her. He helped her family, and she helped him in her own way.

A large, skinny, sunburned white man walked into Shawn's office as soon as she was gone.

"Hey, Shawn, this place is cool. If you have any leftovers, send them my way," he said, nodding in Monica's direction.

Shawn had met Sam Baker at the local market while grocery shopping. Sam was a tech guy, nothing more. Just someone who knew how to install cameras and wire up closed-circuit systems. That was what he was doing now.

Sam had burned out in Silicon Valley working for some big names. He wanted a more laid-back life. He drifted from job to job, smoking marijuana, snorting coke, and dabbling in designer drugs between gigs.

Two soldiers of fortune were setting up their sniper rifles and determining fields of fire in the two bell towers. There was nobody in this country, let alone in this city, who had as much training in shooting, close-quarters combat, and the like as these two men.

Or so they thought.

Why were they loyal to Shawn? It was simple. He was planning another heist, this time on gold mines in Cajamarca. The gold was moved via helicopter from the mines, and Shawn had the means to finance this operation, along with the brains and political savvy to get them safely to another location.

His next move was in Madre de Dios, deep in the jungle. That region was lawless, a kind of Wild West in Peru. With the money he expected to steal, he could hire enough thugs to keep himself protected.

Shawn said he would finance the heist and take fifty percent. The rest would be divided evenly after subtracting the expenses that Shawn was paying upfront.

But of course, Shawn intended to stab them in the back. This was, after all, Shawn. It was what he did. Asking him not to betray someone was like asking a mosquito not to bite.

For now, it was a pleasant fantasy for the two mercenaries, and it kept them from killing him.

Shawn continued typing on his laptop as the priest entered.

Father Benavides had found Shawn intriguing at first, as did everyone else. A tall, handsome American roughing it in the Andes, far from his luxuries. The priest spoke in English, having been educated in Canada.

"Señor, I have heard reports from some of the townspeople that you are not behaving as a man of God should. What is your interest in Mateo? He's only thirteen years old. Have you no shame?"

Shawn looked up from the laptop as if a fly had disturbed him, and he wanted it gone. This priest was the worst kind—one of the people who could not be bought, intimidated, or bullied. He was honest, good, and humble.

But maybe he could be forced to comply.

"Father Benavides. So good to see you again. And how are your family members in Lima, Arequipa, and Madre de Dios? Here, I took some photos of them recently. See?"

Shawn reached into the old wooden desk, a far cry from the one he used at Trufunds, and pulled out three crisp sheets of paper. Each one contained photos of the priest's relatives, their addresses, and private details he had no business knowing. His time on the dark web, albeit expensive, had paid off again. Some people believed that the love of money was the root of all evil, but to Shawn, it was the solution to everything.

Father Benavides shook like he had seen a ghost. "Shawn... how? You will not profit from this. I'll not be intimidated by a coward like you. The Lord rebuke you, Shawn."

"I'm only interested in the soul. For doth it profit a man to gain the world and to lose his soul?" Shawn raised his eyebrows and tilted his head slightly, as if urging the priest to grasp the deeper meaning.

The priest walked out, defeated.

Shawn knew the man would willingly die himself, but not at the cost of his family. He made a quick mental note to ensure Mateo was sent far away—to family in Lima, out of the priest's reach.

There were honest men in Peru, like anywhere else. Men who couldn't be bought or manipulated. Men who wouldn't turn a blind eye out of greed or fear.

But none of them were nearby. Not now. For now, it's damage control, prayer, and preaching.

Shawn couldn't kill Father Benavides. The man was too well-liked. He would be missed immediately. There would be newspaper articles, questions, and outrage. Blatant, cold-blooded murder wouldn't go unnoticed.

For now, the priest lived. That could change.

CHAPTER 25:
TO THE AIRPORT TO MEET HIS FATE

Thursday, 12 February 2015, 0334 hours
Eddy's house, Grapevine, Texas

It was dark in Eddy's room. He liked it that way. Dina slept in his room during the winter months. Eddy was uneasy that night, tossing and turning through strange dreams. When the alarm finally sounded, Eddy was already dressed in his sweatsuit. His nerves had already kicked in. There was no way he could've stayed in bed.

He could feel the new lean muscle he'd built in recent weeks. He hit the floor and banged out a few sets of pushups and sit-ups. There wasn't enough time for a run. He checked in to his flight online and printed his boarding pass. Then he said goodbye to Dina again and texted Claudia, his dog sitter.

The night before, Eddy had disconnected the battery cables to his car to prevent draining while he was gone. He gave the house one last glance while checking his bag again. He'd decided to take only one bag this time. He'd packed his passport, small bills in U.S. and Peruvian currency, electronics, clothes, and the tools needed to tear down computers. He took a photo of everything before zipping it shut.

The Uber arrived at his house before 0530, and Eddy was on his way to the airport. He was traveling internationally but would only fly as far as Miami. From there, he needed to contact Shawn.

Once at the gate, Eddy sat down and checked his phone. There was a message from Claudia reminding him not to worry. She'd take good care of Dina.

The following message was from Shawn.

Eddy, call me when you get this. Give me your flight number and arrival time. I'll have my guy contact you, and you might want to apologize to me for the way you spoke to me last time. I've been waiting for that apology—no need to give you his number. I'll have him call you. Are you ready to make a significant income? Easy sailing, Eddy, work your magic. You're going to love it here. You owe me big time. You really need to try the Ayahuasca. It will open your eyes to new horizons.

Eddy didn't want to call Shawn, but he figured he couldn't get out of this one. He reluctantly selected Shawn's number and hit dial. To his delight, it went straight to voicemail.

"Hi, Shawn, looks like I couldn't get in touch with you. Your pilot should be able to reach me around noon when I'm getting my bags."

To settle his nerves, Eddy scrolled through articles about Peru. Staying busy was his way of handling stress.

You know a lot already, Eddy. Try to relax. Shawn's a bloviator. Be rough with him. When he's angry, he makes mistakes. Force him to get angry. The more mistakes, the better.

His phone rang. He ignored it. He knew that would piss Shawn off. Sure enough, there were new messages.

Shawn: I know you're not on the plane yet. Call me.

Eddy grimaced. You don't demand that I do anything anymore, Shawn. Fuck you.

Eddy breathed in and out with two long breaths.

Let Shawn stew for a while.

CHAPTER 26:
STAY SHARP IN MIAMI

Monday, 12 January 2015, 1125 hours
Miami International Airport, Miami, Florida

Eddy's plane landed slightly ahead of schedule thanks to favorable winds and weather, but Eddy was in no hurry, so he let people push ahead and clear the way for him first.

He made his way down to pick up his bag and pistol case. After dealing with the baggage department that had safeguarded the pistol case, he quickly made his way to the restroom, ignoring a phone call from an unknown number. He was sure it was his mysterious contact in Miami.

Once inside the bathroom and in a closed stall, Eddy made the switch as quickly as he could, pulling out the two firearms he'd decided to bring: his Browning Hi-Power nine-millimeter and the Glock 43 Winston had presented him with.

Eddy had twenty-five rounds of hollow-point ammunition, which would work in both firearms. They fit, albeit tightly, into the space inside the hard Silent Wolf laptop carrier in their secret compartment.

He opened the stall door and waited for the opportunity to stuff the gun case into the trash bin. He couldn't risk leaving the airport with it—someone could be watching him.

Eddy walked to the carousel for his bag. He'd marked it with a long orange tag that he saw slowly moving along. He picked it up and slipped the computer case with the two firearms and ammo inside. Then he texted Shawn.

I'm at terminal C15 baggage claim. When do I meet up with your guy?

Shawn sent back a typically condescending text.

Eddy took this chance to call Pete on one of the burners he'd been given.

The phone rang, then Pete's voice came through. "Hello Eddy, what's the good news, brother?"

"The good news is that I'm closer to serving a little justice to Shawn now. I think his flying ace just called me because it was a Miami number, but I didn't answer. I could tell you I'm not scared, but that would be a lie."

Pete waited a few seconds, then replied, "Hey, look, man, Wise Dog and I have been in Lima for a few days, and we've made some connections. We have some firearms, revolvers. Nothing too fancy, but it's better than nothing. Bad luck, our 7th Group buddies couldn't hook us up because they're otherwise preoccupied. We rented a car since we don't have to be undercover like you. I'm going to need you to hide the burner once you get me a little fidelity on your pilot. If Shawn catches you with the firearms, you can at least say it's for your protection. A burner phone is another story. You shouldn't need one.

When you feel you're in a safe place, use it to call me again."

Eddy was breathing a little hard. "OK, I'll send you a WhatsApp message and erase it on my end after that. Did I forget anything else, O Wise One?"

"I'm not the wise one. That's the Dog. I'm the good-looking one. Just lie low. The psychological profile of this individual suggests he's overly confident. I doubt he's on to you."

Without another word, Pete ended the call in a way Eddy's grandmother would have called rude. That was to say, he didn't even bother to say goodbye.

Oh well, don't judge, Eddy. Everyone says you have terrible table manners.

Eddy made his way through security and looked at the local tourist attractions on the walls.

Well, I'm not just going to sit around twiddling my thumbs, waiting for this guy. I'm going to lie on the beach, maybe swim a little. I don't even know if I'm staying the night here.

It felt like his phone was reading his mind. It rang, and to Eddy's disappointment, it was Shawn. He let it ring three times before he picked up, giving himself time to figure out what to say.

An irritated Shawn came through. "Eddy, look, my guy is a little tied up. Catch a movie or something. He'll call you in a few hours. Next time, pick up faster."

Eddy said, "What was that? I wasn't paying attention to you, Shawn."

"Knock it off, Eddy. You're making a lot of money from me."

"Yes, and I'm doing you a big favor. You need my skills. You don't have anyone else, or you wouldn't be calling me."

Eddy was right, and he knew it. Shawn's silence confirmed it.

Shawn said, "Keep your phone on. He'll be calling you in a few hours."

Yeah, whatever, control freak.

"OK, bye."

Eddy ended the call. He knew it would piss off Shawn.

People can't have power over you unless you give it to them.

OK, now what do I do while I wait? Find a coffee shop, use GPS, and send the coordinates to Pete and Wise Dog. Keep my back against the wall and watch any doors. Communicate through one of the social profiles I created with Pete. Record any calls from numbers I don't recognize. Okay, Eddy, Uber to a good Starbucks and get the computer up and running.

CHAPTER 27:
CONTROLLED TRANSFER

Eddy sat down in the Starbucks with his two venti cappuccinos. *Why waste time getting up to get more?*

The stress was already draining him.

He was chatting with Pete on Facebook. He'd taken the liberty of stashing the burner phone immediately after finishing the call with Shawn and sending Pete a text message telling him he was doing it.

He felt as if people were watching him, even though he'd selected an area on the second floor, and he was alone for the time being.

Eddy heard footsteps approaching on the wooden floor. In the doorway appeared a man who looked like he'd been in his share of fights from the scars on his face, fists, and a nose that looked like it had been broken at least once. Despite his scars, he had a pleasant face. He stood at five feet, nine inches tall and had one of those natural athletic looks that Eddy always envied. This guy did not need to spend hours in the gym to look that way. He just lived his life and worked out occasionally.

The man looked right at him, and for a few seconds, Eddy wished he had access to his firearms. *There is no way I can beat this guy in a fair fight.*

As the man drew closer, a smile began to build on his face. He extended his right hand non-threateningly, and Eddy stood hesitantly to shake it, but not before closing his social media account with three clicks.

"Johnny Croenen," the man said. "Shawn sent me. He said you knew him as 'Shawn.'"

"That's right," Eddy said.

Johnny looked a little apologetic. "Hey man, I'm sorry if I startled you. Toni, I mean Shawn, had me follow you from the airport. He gave me your description."

"*What* description?"

"He sent me some photos of you, and what can I say? The guy has connections." Johnny shrugged, "I'm sorry for all this cloak-and-dagger stuff. I'm not supposed to let you out of my sight, and we fly out tonight ASAP. He wants you at his place before tomorrow morning. He already has a representative meeting with you on the other end, who will take care of the customs paperwork so that you can move through the process quickly. Any questions?"

Well, at least I'm being treated as a special prisoner. "No, thanks. Just let me pack up, and we can get going."

Eddy slowly put his stuff away, trying to figure out how he would signal to Pete what had happened, *probably on my iPhone from the hangar.*

Johnny didn't act like he suspected Eddy of anything, so there were no issues there.

They hopped into Johnny's Ford F-150 pickup truck and headed to the hangar. Eddy was tortured by heavy metal music for most of the way, with Johnny telling dirty jokes.

Once inside, Johnny introduced Eddy to his fiancée, Miriami Morales, who didn't have much to say to him. However, she surprised him with some good home-cooked food. Miriami made spaghetti and meatballs, and a nice salad. Eddy drank red wine, but Johnny and Miriami were the pilots, so they didn't have any.

After the meal, Eddy used the small restroom inside the hangar. While the water was running, he IMed Pete on Messenger to explain what had happened and tell him everything he'd figured out, which wasn't much.

How could Pete and Wise Dog follow him from the airport now? He sent the tail number to Pete but doubted that it would help much.

Eddy had the tracking device from Silent Wolf, but that wouldn't tell Pete where he was headed, just where he was. He decided to turn it on. With a click of a nice ballpoint pen, Eddy was being tracked. He knew this would keep up until the battery died in about forty-eight hours. He figured if he weren't dead by then, the tracker wouldn't be necessary, anyway. Knowing Shawn, he wouldn't want to be too far away from the creature comforts of a city.

At 2013 hours, Miriami walked in. "OK, Eddy, we're leaving in twenty."

Johnny grabbed his gear and sat with Eddy to watch him.

Once onboard, Eddy was able to get some sleep.

The three arrived in Lima at 0217 hours on Tuesday, 13 February 2015. It was the same skip-and-dance routine as with Shawn and his crew.

There was a well-muscled man in an older model Honda Accord who looked like the poster boy for "Mercs are Us." Eddy recognized the tattoos as those of someone who had spent time in the United States Special Forces. He was curt but not mean.

"Hey Eddy, I'm Frederico. Shawn has me chauffeuring you. We should be there in time for breakfast."

Eddy started to object, but Frederico pulled up his untucked shirt and revealed a semiautomatic Sig Sauer pistol on his belt. Eddy was afraid of this intimidating-looking man, who was also packing a firearm, while Eddy's weapon was inside his laptop case. With that, the man turned his gaze away from Eddy and focused on his bag. Eddy loaded it into the trunk of the Honda, and off they went.

OK, so it looks like the plan for using Pete's driver went right out the window, Eddy thought. Please, God, let that pen tracker work.

Eddy tried to strike up a conversation with Frederico, but Frederico was not interested. Instead, he thought about the task ahead. *I can take Shawn in a fight, but not this guy. Frederick would wipe the floor with me. The best I could hope for would be to get a lucky shot in or two. Well, only if the guy didn't fight back.*

Eddy pulled out his phone to contact Pete, but Frederico shook his head, wagging his finger. Shawn might not have been on to Eddy, but he certainly wasn't taking any chances.

After two restroom stops and an upset stomach, they were in Huancayo. The city appeared dirty to Eddy, probably because it was. There was trash in the streets. *Not the most touristy place, but maybe a good place for Shawn to hide,* Eddy thought. *Although he would stand out as a gringo here. I wonder what he's using for cover. Probably the old Reverend Shawn thing again.*

CHAPTER 28:
INTO MY PARLOUR SAID
THE SPIDER TO THE FLY

Friday, 13 February 2015, 0817 hours
Shawn's headquarters, Huancayo, Peru

The old, rusted brown Honda pulled up to the church that, on the outside, looked to be of the same color as the Honda, intermixed with off-white and off-red. Eddy was a little puzzled by this.

Is this guy going to stop and pray or what? Don't tell me he's one of Shawn's converts.

Frederico finally broke the long silence. "Your home, Wildman! No rest for the weary. Shawn wants you to start work right after breakfast. You're going to have to earn your pay."

Eddy said, "How did you guys acquire your own church down here?"

Frederico replied, "Too many questions, Sherlock. You're being paid to do computer stuff, not interrogate us. Talk to Shawn. Other than that, have a nice day, asshole."

Frederico popped the trunk with a button under the dashboard. He feigned a smile, showing as many of his teeth as he could.

Out of the old church walked a man of about 6'3". From a distance, Eddy could see that the man was taller than the others standing outside. Eddy recognized that slow, almost lazy gait, and the hands in front of him, which oddly didn't move when he walked.

As the man came closer, Eddy could see that he had a sneaky smile and an appearance that some would consider fashionable. His hair was immaculate, and he walked with an air of authority. In place of a shirt, he wore a large black Japanese-style jacket decorated with butterflies, and he held a lit cigar in his right hand.

He wore shorts, and on his feet were white slippers. There could be no doubt that it was Shawn, although he had lost a few pounds due to his carefree lifestyle, lack of work, and self-discipline. There were a few local people standing close to him.

"Hi, buddy!" Shawn embraced Eddy.

"So, we don't talk for almost four years, and now you need something," Eddy interjected. "I get it, but I'm here for the money, Shawn. Remember that. Then I'm outta here and whatever shady stuff you're involved in."

"I'm sorry you feel that way, Eddy. I never did anything wrong to you. But you are not perfect either; you must remember that. Remember, 'Judge not lest you be judged.'"

Eddy said, "Whatever. Got anything to eat around here? And what's with me not being allowed to use my phone? I'm not in jail. You hired me to do a job, and I'm going to do it."

"Calm down. It's not good for the digestion to argue before a meal," Shawn said. "Take your bag inside. I converted one of the offices into a room for you. After we eat, we can get right to work."

Eddy noted Shawn's resourcefulness in having procured a church building. It offered excellent protection from small arms fire, good visibility, and a wide field of fire for a rifle, and it had secure locks and ample space. He knew Pete and Wise Dog would be looking for him. He needed to stall Shawn a little to give them time to zero in on his location.

"Alright, man. Let me get a shower first, and then I need like two cups of coffee if I'm putting in a full day."

Shawn frowned but conceded. "This way."

Shawn hurried up the path, handing the cigar to one of the locals, who apparently worked for him. "I estimate, with your skills, this should take no more than a few days."

Eddy was nervous. The situation wasn't natural. He told himself he was overthinking it, as he often did.

He said, "That's optimistic. I'm not even sure what the real problem is here. What I can tell you is that by the end of the day tomorrow, I should at least know what's going on and estimate how long it will take to fix it."

Shawn wasn't paying attention. He was talking to some church workers carrying heavy metal boxes.

He saw Frederico and another mercenary walking together with the familiar outline of pistols underneath their clothing. Both headed up the stairs to a tower, saying something about clearing fields of fire.

In his room, Eddy unpacked his bags and grabbed a spare set of clothes. Nothing fancy, jeans and a T-shirt, underwear, and socks. He caught a man passing by and asked for directions to the shower.

"I'll show you."

The man was carrying tools that were familiar to Eddy: computer tools, small screwdrivers, and various connectors and wires, things that someone who did this for a living would have.

The man extended his hand. "Sam, Sam Baker," Sam explained, he was another tech guy on Shawn's team. He hadn't had any luck cracking the hard drive yet, which made Eddy more anxious.

When they arrived at the small bathroom, Eddy saw no towel or washcloth for him. *Screw it,* he thought.

He showered in lukewarm water and dried himself with his old clothes. He flossed, brushed his teeth, and returned to his room with his dirty clothes in a trash bag.

He heard movement in the kitchen area and smelled the aroma of food. That was where they were meeting this morning. He could hear the eggs frying, and the smell of bacon and coffee filled the air. *Well, at least I'll eat well here.*

Eddy entered the kitchen, where two hired guns sat at the table, reminiscing about their days in the military. Of all things, they were comparing head shots.

It was apparent both were former army from the tattoos they sported and the places they'd served.

Shawn was still smoking his cigar and sipping coffee. He raised both eyebrows as a hello to Eddy and then returned to his conversation with the two mercenaries. Something about security was needed to pull off a job in Cajamarca. And gold.

Frederico nodded in greeting. The other man rolled his eyes at Eddy and said, "Name's Manuel. Shawn tells me you're a Lieutenant Colonel in the United States Army. I did almost all my time down in South America training illiterate toothless motherfuckers. What's your branch[5]?"

What an idiot. Some of the greatest minds in the world come from here. "Well, I started enlisted in tanks and then switched over to the officer side of the house. I did fourteen years in the Military Police and then I branch transferred to Intelligence."

Manuel gave him a disparaging expression. "Wow, a secret squirrel," he said sarcastically. "They don't want to get their hands dirty." The two mercenaries shared a knowing look, the way some look at the slow kid in class who didn't quite get it. It was clear they thought of themselves as better than Eddy. The Alpha Males in the room.

---

5   The Army, Navy, Air Force, Marines, etc., are called branches. Within the Army, officers also have a branch. That can be Infantry, Artillery, Military Police, Military Intelligence, etc.

Manuel continued, "I heard about that shot you made in Afghanistan. Can you teach me to shoot like that?" More sarcasm.

"Yeah, and I'll teach you how to read too, if you have the time between lifting weights and taking steroids," Eddy shot back.

Frederico laughed at Manuel.

Shawn said, "Hey, guys, take it easy on him. He's here to do a job for me. Eddy, grab some coffee. Tell me about your trip."

Eddy sat and poured himself a cup of coffee, and the local chef placed eggs on his plate, along with two slices of bacon and toast.

"There's not much to tell. Johnny just about kidnapped me from Starbucks after following me there. Then, I was under house arrest with Johnny and his girlfriend, Ms. Congeniality, until the flight took off. Oh yeah, then I sat next to Friendly Frederico there on the luxurious drive up here and had a pleasant time. We had some in-depth conversations. He even allowed me to stop and use the bathroom twice, but no cell phones were allowed. If I'm your friend, how do you treat your enemies, Shawn?" Eddy said.

Shawn nodded to the chef, who left the room. He was clearly thinking of something else as the three men looked at him for a rebuttal that never came.

Finally, Eddy spoke up again. "Well, I need to lie down for a little while. My head is spinning with all this traveling. It isn't even ten o'clock in the morning yet. I have the time to figure out your stuff. I promise, I won't try to run off." It was true. Eddy was dead tired.

Shawn said, "OK, go lie down for a few hours. Everyone, leave him alone for a while and let his batteries recharge."

Eddy wolfed down the rest of his food.

Once back in his room, he pulled out the burner phone and sent a message to Pete on social media.

Pete, I made it. Two tough-looking SPECOPS guys are Shawn's fighters. He has some locals for a cook and a few servants. There is a gringo wandering around who looks like a handyman who has some basic computer skills. I need to get some shut-eye.

Pete didn't respond.

After the text, a thought entered Eddy's mind. I hope he's not responding because he doesn't want to blow my cover.

CHAPTER 29:
UNDER WATCHFUL EYES

Friday, 13 February 2015, 1532 hours
Eddy's room, Huancayo, Peru

When Eddy woke up, his throat was parched, and he reached for a water bottle from his bedside. He looked at his phone. There was a message from Pete under the profile he'd created. He read it.

Having a great time in Connecticut. Currently, we're in the main square and can see what we want from here.

OK, Pete was in Huancayo and had eyes on him! Well, that gave him some reassurance, at least. *I've stalled Shawn long enough.*

Eddy realized he had no option but to begin work on the project he was hired to do. Although Sam wasn't in the same league as him, he would notice if Eddy was stalling too much. Progress had to be made—time to find Shawn and get to work.

He checked his computer equipment and weapons in the case and decided he didn't need the burner phone. He took the Glock, ejected the magazine, and loaded it. He concealed it the way Winston had shown him, with the holster down in his crotch. He didn't know if he would be searched or how often it would happen.

Eddy left his room and called out, "Hey Shawn, where are you at, man? I've got work to do, remember?"

He followed Shawn's voice to a door and knocked on it.

Sure enough, Shawn appeared at the door wearing the same Japanese jacket. Behind him, a Peruvian woman lay in the bed, who looked to be under the influence of something, as her eyes were glazed over.

She's stoned out of her mind.

The room was rather large and colorful.

Shawn said, "Sandra and I were just doing some catching up. Great, this way, brother."

Shawn walked down the hall to a room with several locks on its door. Once opened, Eddy realized the room had no windows. However, it had a high ceiling with two openings, making it a little less stuffy.

A workbench and two wooden chairs were in the center of the room.

"OK, this is your new work area. You can keep your computer stuff here. Manuel and Frederico will take turns keeping you secure."

Yeah, more like babysitting me and making sure I don't steal anything or run away.

Eddy said, "Yeah, man, let me go grab my stuff and I'll be right back. Put my prison guards on alert."

Shawn frowned at this but didn't respond. Instead, he pulled out a walkie-talkie and said, "Manuel, Fred, sleeping beauty is awake and working. Keep him fed and happy, but make sure he keeps working." Looking at

Eddy, he said, "Oh yeah, I almost forgot." He produced two large Cuban cigars from the right pocket of his large black jacket. "This is a smoking area, so feel free to indulge. I also know you like your coffee, so we'll keep it flowing. Mr. Baker has been busy setting up the electricity here, so you should have plenty of power, and the lighting will suffice for now. Get comfortable and keep me updated twice daily. Once in the morning, around noon, and then again around six in the evening."

"Yes, Mommy Dearest," Eddy replied as sarcastically as he could, knowing it would irritate Shawn.

He hurried back to retrieve his gear, pulled the burner phone out of its hiding place, and sent as accurate a description as he could on social media of the room's location.

Eddy removed the Glock from his waistband and replaced it with the burner phone. He extracted the Browning Hi-Power from the compartment, ejected the magazine, and loaded it. Taking duct tape, he crawled under the bed and taped the Glock there. A child playing might find it, but it was unlikely anyone else would.

He returned the Browning Hi-Power nine-millimeter pistol to the compartment.

Eddy returned to the workroom, stopping at the kitchen for bottled water, coffee, and snacks. He set his gear on the sturdy bench and got to work. If Shawn were being brought to justice, it wouldn't matter if he solved his computer problems, and even impatient Shawn would have to admit that Eddy needed a few days to fix this. After all, nobody else here could, right?

He had his tools set out on the bench when Shawn returned and opened the safe. Inside it was a hard drive that held 4MB of data.

"OK, dude, here's the deal. I can't access my crypto because this key has a security feature that I can't figure out how to bypass. Your job is to break the code as soon as possible. The sooner you do it, the sooner you get paid. We have Friday Bible study 'Nuggets of God's Love' tomorrow at six, so it would be good if you could get it done by then."

Eddy frowned. "That's pushing it, Shawn. I need a few days."

I need to give Pete and Wise Dog time to execute their plans.

Pete told Eddy that Cecilia at Trufunds had placed software on this key at Mr. Ortiz's request, and Eddy could access it, but it would take hours because the failsafe wouldn't deactivate immediately, and now there were security measures in place that would take hours to fix. Not even Cecilia could have done it quicker.

Shawn said, "OK, just keep me updated. I expect progress."

It was Manuel who watched Eddy first. He didn't stay in the room with Eddy but sat in a comfortable chair outside the door. This gave Eddy an idea. He moved his tools around, making sure to make plenty of noise.

Sounding busy, he pulled out the roll of duct tape and cut several pieces into six-inch strands.

Eddy heard footsteps and went to the door to listen for their movement, but they continued past his door and on down the hall. He tiptoed around to the back of the safe and found there was ample room to secure the Browning with tape. Eddy didn't know when the gunfight would happen, but he knew where to access at least one firearm. He shoved the burner phone into his left-side cargo pocket.

Manuel was looking at his phone. He looked up. "What's up, hotshot?"

"I need a little fresh air." Eddy said, "Can someone show me around this place? I mean, it is not like I'm going to come here every year."

Manuel replied, "OK, Goldilocks, since you're the golden boy for now, I'll have Sam take you for a walk. Keep it under an hour, got it?"

"You bet," Eddy said.

Manuel called Sam on the radio. He was working on an air conditioner in Shawn's office, a luxury here.

A minute later, Sam showed up sweaty, wearing shorts and a Megadeth t-shirt.

"Let's go, partner. I'm going to give you the twenty-five-cent tour."

They walked out together, each carrying a bottle of water. Eddy asked, "So, how did you wind up with Shawn?" They exited the church and there were some people outside, including vendors and couples walking around. Some of the people looked at Eddy and Sam a little longer as there were almost no gringos in this town.

"It was easy." Sam replied, "I was staying at a hostel here and not doing much outside of playing my guitar. I speak English and passable Spanish, and I have some technical skills he needed, so he hired me. I just take the cash."

"Fair enough. I went to the University in Texas with him. He was always very popular with friends and girlfriends. I worked for him for a while, but he didn't pay so well then, and he wasn't such a great boss either."

Sam said, "Well, anyway, this town is a tourism spot for Peruvians, but not for foreigners. We stand out here. Shawn is a missionary, among other things, so they accept him, kind of, but he still gets looks. I came here to get away—ex-wife, high-stress job, high expectations from my family. Back home, life was all about keeping up with other people. The best cars. The nicest houses. Gym time. Watches. Jewelry. I mean, what's the point? Enjoy your life. Time to live a little for me and stop meeting other people's requirements. I sold it all and decided to do the backpacking thing for a while."

Eddy smiled. "I like the way you said that. Let's get something to eat. I'm buying. I want to try some of that ceviche stuff."

"Sure. I know a nice place."

They walked down a side street to a ceviche restaurant. Both had some chicha de jora, a fermented drink made from corn. Eddy pulled out the cell phone and called Pete while Sam not-so-subtly admired a woman walking by.

Sam looked at Eddy suspiciously and nodded to the cell phone.

Eddy said, "Look, man, I have to call my girlfriend, or she's going to get worried."

Unfortunately, the call went to voicemail.

Eddy left a message. "Hey, Hon, you were right. Man, it's different here in Peru. The sun is intense here. I already suffered heat in two different locations, but I found a hiding place where I can get relative coolness."

He was letting Pete know that the firearms were in two different locations. "I'm going to be doing Bible Study tomorrow evening with Shawn at six, and it's over at seven, so I'll grab whatever I can afterwards. Love ya."

They finished their meal, and Eddy said, "Well, the time police told me to return in under an hour."

They had been gone about forty-five minutes, and it was 1732 hours.

Eddy and Sam talked a little on the way back, with Sam pointing out things and Eddy noticing the dirty streets. He'd read that there was good hiking in the Nevado mountain range, as well as other tourist attractions, but the lack of attention to sanitation could ruin everything.

When they returned, Sam headed back to Shawn's office, and Eddy returned to his work area. He'd taken a chance putting the firearm behind the safe like that, but he was counting on Shawn remembering that Eddy wasn't a risk-taker.

Eddy noted the door was made of metal, solid, and at least three inches thick. He was sure it would repel small arms fire. That could come in handy in the next twenty-four hours or so.

Before entering the office, Eddy saw that Frederico was guarding the room now. He saw a Sig Sauer pistol in a brown leather holster strapped across his chest and a pump-action Remington shotgun leaning against the wall close to him.

Eddy and Frederico exchanged cold, brief nods without a word, and Eddy entered the office to start troubleshooting again. He performed cursory clean-ups of the hard drive to improve its efficiency. However, because Shawn's crew had messed with the key, it would take hours to access the code, something that Eddy was grateful for as it bought him time.

Nobody had given Eddy the key, and that was by design. The drive, a compact 4MB unit with custom firmware, was built for one purpose: to hold a single, encrypted file under strict conditions.

After multiple failed access attempts, the protection software activated, tightening the system's defenses. By the time Eddy was called in, others had already spent weeks trying to bypass it without success.

Eddy started by cloning the drive, preserving the original image in case the system responded unpredictably. From there, he scanned for entropy patterns and structural irregularities. He found an obfuscated file fragment masked with a basic XOR layer. Removing that revealed what looked like the beginning of a Wallet Import Format key, but the rest of it was locked down with PBKDF2 encryption, salted, iterated, and deliberately slow to crack.

He had the passphrase already. Eddy didn't need to break anything, but he was in no rush. *My job was to oversee the process and maintain appearances.*

Eddy kept the screen busy with terminal windows, status reports, and checksum verifications. All legitimate tools, all running slow enough to look like progress. No one needed to know how far along he was.

He did not have a large ego, but he knew he was the best and could crack this. He just didn't want to. He wanted to do just enough so his intentions weren't questioned.

Eddy said, "OK, Mr. Bodyguard, may I be excused for the evening?"

Manuel frowned and grabbed his radio. "Hey, Shawn, little Eddy wants a break for his beauty rest."

Shawn appeared a moment later, walking briskly down the hall. "What's the good news, my friend?"

Eddy gave him a tight smile. "The good news is, I know a lot of things this isn't. I'll try some experimental software tomorrow. Might have it cracked by Thursday morning, give or take."

I won't even begin the process until the afternoon, in case it works too well.

Shawn nodded. "As long as you get it done. Help yourself to breakfast in the morning."

He might be a bastard, but he is a civilized bastard.

"Oh, and Eddy, you need to concentrate on your work. Keep your phone in your laptop case and put it in the safe. You can pick it up when you're done. Sam told me you called your girlfriend. She'll just have to wait."

I can't trust Sam to keep his mouth shut. Noted.

Eddy rolled his eyes. He dropped the iPhone into the inside pocket of the carrying case, grateful he'd removed the pistols from the case. It would be suspiciously heavy with two guns and ammunition.

Shawn locked up the safe with Eddy's computer things inside.

Thank God for the burner phone.

Eddy went to the kitchen and grabbed a glass of whiskey. He walked across the street and sat on a bench. He cut off the end of the cigar with a cutter and expertly lit the Cuban cigar with a match. Eddy alternated between puffs on the cigar and sipping the whiskey.

He surveyed his surroundings.

It was dark by then. Even if he was being watched, he doubted they would see the burner phone, even if he put it on speaker and kept it on his lap. He was a boring person to begin with, and nobody paid much attention to him. This worked in his favor.

Eddy called Don, who picked up on the second ring. It was the same time in Florida at Don's house as it was in Peru.

Barely audible, Don said, "Hello?"

Eddy spoke quietly, almost in a whisper. "Hi, Don, this is Eddy. I'm using a burner phone. Sorry to call you so late. You know, I normally wouldn't. In fact, I'd normally be trying to go to bed right now. I left Pete a message. I'm in place at a church in Huancayo. Pete knows the one. There are just three entrances that I know of: the main church entrance and one back entrance, and I'm not sure how hard it is to get into the side entrance. The best time to strike is after the end of Bible study tomorrow at 1900, possibly closer to 1920. Wait until all the people are gone. I'll be back in the small room he has me working in. I have a piece hidden there, and it's loaded. He has two goons, and they're good. Special ops of course, but we have the element of surprise on our side, and they won't count on me putting up a fight. The whole intel image, you know."

Don said, "I'll call Pete and let him know. You're going to be fine, dude. You hang in there, buddy. Hey, Eddy, how much of this is for money and justice, and how much is to get closure for your issues with this guy?"

"These guys aren't dumb, Don," Eddy responded. "Now you know the time, and Pete knows the place because he tailed me here with GPS. That's all you need to know. I'm ditching this phone—it's a liability."

Eddy ended the call without saying goodbye. He was extremely nervous.

CHAPTER 30:
FACE YOUR DEMONS

Wednesday, 14 January 2015, 0527 hours
Eddy's room, Huancayo, Peru

Eddy was awake before his alarm went off; it was his nerves, and understandable in a place where they would kill him if they knew what was going on.

Maybe they'll kill me before this whole thing happens anyway, he thought. I need to keep them happy and calm for the next thirteen and one-half hours. After that, it won't matter. He'd never killed anyone 'on purpose.' The Taliban commander "Ghost One" was a complete screw-up on his part. He should have received a reprimand, not a Bronze Star. Could he look someone in the face and do it if he had to? I hope Pete and Wise Dog do all the fighting, but what if I have no choice?

Eddy went for a run, followed by a round of calisthenics, then took a shower and got dressed for the day.

By the time he walked into the kitchen, it was 0810 hours. Manuel and Frederico were busy devouring eggs and bacon, telling dirty jokes, and competing for the biggest liar award. The normal macho banter between two Alphas, each wanting to be the top dog.

Eddy said, "Howdy fellas, how's it hanging?"

Frederico replied, "A lot harder and a lot longer and bigger than yours, professor."

"Have you been sneaking peeks at me in the shower again, Fred? You really ought to talk to someone about that."

That earned him a dirty look from Frederico and a laugh and nod from Manuel as if to say, "You got him."

Frederico was working on his comeback when Shawn entered, yawning and stretching. This time, he was fully dressed.

He must have business to attend to this morning.

"You children look nice." Shawn said, "We have work to do."

The local chef, Ricardo, had just returned from getting groceries for lunch or "Almuerzo." They had it later than in the U.S.—typically 1300 and often at 1500. He had his assistant, Leo, helping this morning.

Leo said, "What would you gentlemen like to have?"

Eddy felt the need for a bit of assertiveness to have more control. He said, "Well, I have some work to do, and I need energy. I would like three fried eggs, three pieces of bacon, two pieces of toast with butter, orange juice, and a lot of coffee. I'll help myself to the fruit on the table."

Shawn looked at Eddy with irritation, and his nose curled to the right as it often did when he was upset. "Dude, this isn't just a vacation. Where is my status update?"

Wow, there he goes again, establishing dominance.

He responded with a sneer, "Yes, Mother Dearest. But if you want miracles, maybe don't treat me like dirt."

"Fortune favors the bold, Eddy. And for what I'm paying you, you'd better be really bold. I would like it done today, and I would like to know the status before Bible Study. That money is to help me spread God's word; it is important."

Manuel and Frederico rolled their eyes when Shawn wasn't looking.

Sam entered, looking a little hungover. His eyes were bloodshot, he clearly had not shaved, and his clothes were disheveled and a little dirty. Eddy was reminded of the countless people he'd encountered on his travels who just didn't really fit in anywhere and self-medicated with alcohol and party drugs. Sam wasn't a bad guy, just a guy who had been given some bad breaks in life and was looking to make things better. He wasn't stupid enough to believe that Shawn and his crew were innocent, but it was unlikely that he knew the extent of their evil deeds.

An unfamiliar female voice came from Shawn's bedroom. "Shawn, I'm hungry. Can you bring me something, please?"

Shawn snapped to get Leo's attention. "Take care of that for me."

"Coming right up, boss!" Leo turned to attend to the orders.

Shawn returned to his room, and the rest remained in the kitchen, except the chef, The chef also doubled as a janitor for the church, earning some additional income on top of his cheffing duties.

Frederico, Manuel, Eddy, and Sam sat, mostly in silence, checking their phones, except for Eddy, who wasn't allowed to have one. The chef served each of them their breakfast. They ate and observed each other's behaviors for about fifteen minutes and left—first, the two bodyguards, followed by Eddy, and finally Sam.

It was just before nine when Eddy asked his minders for permission to enter his work area. They complied, and Manuel politely knocked on Shawn's door and asked him to open the safe.

"Shawn, pause whatever you have going on in here and let our guest get his stuff so we can get rid of him. He's starting to get on our nerves."

Shawn answered, "I'll be right out."

As usual, it took Shawn longer than he said. There was feminine giggling inside the room, and he finally made his way out nearly half an hour later. "Took you long enough," Eddy said, irritated.

Shawn shrugged, "Not my problem. Work faster, skip lunch, whatever. Get it done. I don't care how."

Eddy needed to initiate the actual process today so that Shawn could access his money. He didn't know how long it would take, but he needed to report progress. If Eddy interrupted his Bible Study to tell him it's done, Shawn wouldn't be able to concentrate; he might even wrap it up early. *I'll get him into this room before Pete and Dog strike. I need to have the gun ready and hidden somewhere accessible.*

"Fine. Have Ricardo bring my lunch here then, so I can meet your deadline."

This is going to be a long day.

Eddy hooked up all the nerdy equipment, got online, and started the process. He glanced around the corner and saw that Manuel was using headphones, listening to heavy metal, and surfing the web on his phone.

Now's my chance.

Eventually, Frederico relieved Manuel, and Shawn stopped him as he was walking down the hall. They discussed something Eddy couldn't understand. He heard things being moved and the familiar sound of weapons being locked and loaded.

Shawn popped his head around the corner. "Tick tock, Eddy. Time is money. We are going to run some errands and will be back in time for Bible Study. We have some local people I pay to watch the place when we are low on security. You will see them walking around periodically. Not real professionals, but they'll let us know if anything is wrong, so don't get any funny ideas."

Shawn turned and walked toward the front door, and Eddy could hear the footsteps of others walking away.

A vehicle started, and Eddy recognized it as the SUV from the previous day. He assumed it was Manuel and Shawn who headed away to do whatever mischief they were up to.

Eddy worked for two hours before he needed a restroom break.

Now I'll get ready for the fireworks tonight.

He moved the pistol from where he'd taped it and put it in his right cargo pocket, hoping it would go unnoticed.

Then he looked at Frederico. "Hey, Super Soldier, I need to make a pit stop, please."

"You know where it is. I'm not holding your hand."

The restroom was located to the right, near the entrance, while Frederico sat to the left. Eddy exited the room, careful not to reveal his right side to Frederico.

Once inside the restroom, he pulled the gun out and charged a round into the chamber. He swapped it to his left pocket to hide it from Frederico on his way back. Frederico just looked at him with all the enthusiasm that one shows a passing car during a normal stroll.

Eddy entered the workroom, switched the pistol back to his right pocket, and continued his work.

He was breaking through the security measures that were set on the cloned version of the drive he'd made. He felt that in a few hours, he would have the actual cryptocurrency key.

Eddy sent social media messages to Pete, telling him what was going on. Pete and Wise Dog could take the place now with no issues, but they couldn't risk letting Shawn find out, or he might escape or die fighting. The over five million dollars that was wired went to multiple accounts and remains untraceable so far, thanks to the algorithm.

By 1645, Eddy had cracked the code and obtained the key for the cryptocurrency. He had surprised even himself.

He set up a defragmentation program on the hard drive that would take about ninety minutes.

That'll do the trick. I'll tell Shawn that once this is finished, we'll have the key.

At 1713, he heard Shawn's voice by the front door. Eddy stuffed some of his tools into his pockets to conceal the firearm.

Shawn said, "We'll do this job and then part ways. Even cut for all of you. You earned it!"

No doubt they will believe him, though. By the time they figure him out, it'll be too late. He's that good. There would be no cut for them.

Frederico shouted, "Get the fuck in here, Manuel! I have to take a leak. What did you do? Walk the whole way?"

"Yeah, yeah, here I come. Calm down, man."

While the two of them switched places, Eddy figured out what to say to Shawn.

Shawn came directly to him. "Give me your status."

"After Bible Study, I have a gift for you, Shawn," Eddy said enthusiastically.

Shawn beamed. "Mr. Computer here is earning his pay! Don't fuck with him. He's our golden goose." There were grunts from around the corridor in agreement.

Got him anxious. Maybe now he'll finally shut his freaking mouth so we can make this thing work.

Shawn didn't say anything else to Eddy, but he popped his head in intermittently, and Eddy couldn't risk any more social media messages.

This is where the rubber meets the road.

CHAPTER 31:
THE CALM BEFORE THE GRAB

Saturday, 14 February 2015, 1750 hours
Eddy's workroom, Huancayo, Peru

Shawn stood in the doorway, eyes locked on Eddy like he was reading tells at a poker table. Manuel had dragged a chair into position with a perfect view of the room. All Eddy could do was pretend to work and wait.

"I'm not going to move faster just because you're watching," Eddy said. "Go do your Bible study. I'll tell you when it's ready."

Shawn frowned but said nothing. People were arriving. His performance mattered.

About thirty men and women entered the church. Tired faces, worn clothes. Lives weathered by hardship. Leo moved between them, handing out bowls of food and mugs of tea.

Shawn didn't speak Spanish well enough to preach. Marcus, a local with calm authority, translated each sentence cleanly. The room gave him its full attention.

Shawn lifted his hands. "Brothers and sisters, I feel the Lord moving me to help this congregation. Each of you will receive 100 soles, not as charity, but as a blessing to pass forward. And this Sunday, after church, we'll host a barbecue. Come hungry, and bring your friends."

ss$$$$ss

Eddy watched the laptop. Process complete.

He opened a burner account and typed.

Cracked the code. Bible Study in progress. 1833. Ends 1900—no access to drinks. I'll try again later.

Pete responded a moment later.

Can you isolate him? Clear the civilians or get him outside. Don't give him time to think. Snatch and grab. We hit hard. His guards don't matter. Shawn's the objective. We'll get codes and wire info en route or at Silent Wolf. I don't have his clearance, so we use what we've got. Surprise is the edge. Do not screw it up.

Eddy paused for a moment before responding.

He's into cigars. I'll try that. No guarantees.

"Dude," Manuel barked. "Are you working or what?"

Eddy closed the window. "Yeah. Good news for Shawn. He can access the money."

Manuel shrugged. "Great. Maybe now you'll finally leave. You grow on people like a fungus. Go tell him."

Eddy ignored the jab. He scribbled a note, slid it into his cargo pocket, and left.

The church entrance was crowded. Bible Study was in full swing.

Shawn looked up. His face lit up like a spoiled kid on Christmas morning.

"I'd like you all to meet my good friend Eddy from the States," he said. "He's helping with a technical issue and enjoying your beautiful country."

Eddy flashed a thumbs-up and nodded toward the exit. "One last step," he said. "Fifteen minutes, max. Come outside. I brought whiskey and cigars."

"I need to stay with the flock," Shawn said. "Go ahead. I'll follow shortly."

Eddy stepped into the night. His watch read 1850. The stars were out, but he didn't look up.

What if this all went to hell right now?

He sat on the bench, unwrapped the cigar, and clipped the tip with shaking hands. The blade slipped and nearly cut him. He took a sip of water and forced himself to take a deep breath.

The door creaked behind him.

"What in the fuck are you doing?" Manuel snapped. "You're not supposed to be—"

Pete stepped out of the dark and hit him. His left hook cracked against Manuel's jaw. The sound was wet and final. Manuel dropped. Pete caught him mid-fall.

"Grab his feet."

They hauled him around the building quickly and quietly. A black Range Rover sat a hundred yards away. Pete clicked the fob, and the hatch opened with a soft thump.

"I thought we were waiting until after the Bible Study?" Eddy said. His voice was tight.

"Target of opportunity," Pete muttered. "We're light on firepower. Taking one out now improves our odds."

He zip-tied Manuel's wrists and ankles, gagged him with masking tape, and tapped the pistol on his hip.

"One less variable. Shawn might still come out. Wise Dog's inside. Picked the lock ten minutes ago."

CHAPTER 32:
THE RUBBER MEETS THE ROAD

Saturday, 14 February 2015, 1750 hours
Shawn's headquarters, Huancayo, Peru

Eddy ran back to the church. He swiped the sweat from his brow and eased the door open. Shawn's voice echoed from the sanctuary in English, followed by a Spanish translation. By then, the congregation had already left.

Shawn was laying it on thick with the Huancayo chief of police.

"Thank you, Romeo. Cajamarca hasn't been cooperative in giving me access to information on the Yamacocha mining operation. God wants me to minister to those people. I can feel His pull on my heart. They need a chaplain on the ground every day."

Romeo nodded, clearly pleased with himself. "It's my honor to help you, my friend. Your generous donations to the department have allowed us to give raises to people who haven't had one in years."

Eddy moved quickly, his boots silent against the tile, and ducked into his workspace.

A minute later, he rattled the doorknob just enough to get Shawn's attention.

As Eddy walked toward the sanctuary, he saw a group of about fifty people making their way to the exit.

Their eyes met. Eddy didn't flinch. Shawn broke away from Romeo, a flicker of urgency on his face.

"Eddy! Is it done, bro?"

"It's done." Eddy smiled. "Let's light a cigar. Then I'll walk you through it."

Shawn grinned but shook his head. "No, I want to see it now."

"OK. Just need to grab my water bottle and lighter. I left them outside," Eddy lied.

"All right. Get your stuff and hurry back."

Darn. I was hoping to get him outside. We could have taken him right then.

Eddy stopped in his workspace and stashed the 4MB drive with the crypto key in a pocket. He moved past Manuel, who barely looked up. He was smirking, like he knew something no one else did.

Eddy peeked into the sanctuary. The last civilian had left. Good.

Outside, he scanned the courtyard, one hand hovering near his pocket, then grabbed the sun-warmed water bottle and took a long drink. He pulled a second bottle from his cargo pocket and poured in the sedative.

Pete was on watch. Eddy raised his thumb, slow and deliberate.

A dog barked in the distance. Then silence.

The sun was already starting to drop, but there was still too much daylight for Eddy's comfort. *Surprise is our edge. But they've got better firepower.*

Eddy squared his shoulders. Some battles don't knock. They barge in.

He looked left. Wise Dog had slipped up on him.

"You're really good at that," Eddy said. "Here's the key." He hesitated for the briefest moment, then handed over the drive.

Wise Dog nodded. "Good work. I'll secure the drive in the vehicle. You head back in, keep him calm. Then Pete and I will go in. I'll pick the back lock. Pete takes the front. We retrieve Shawn's bank information. Check the time. We move at 1930."

"Why not now? The parishioners are gone," Eddy said.

Wise Dog motioned for Eddy to slow down. "He's only got two guys like Pete and me, but they're armed better. He also has some locals who frequent the area. If you get him to drink the water, he drops. Then we handle the others without having to shoot our way in."

Eddy didn't like it, but there was no other option. "OK."

He reached the door and waited, chest rising and falling.

Shawn greeted him with a smug grin. "So here we are. The moment of truth."

Eddy's nerves kicked hard.

I don't even have the key. If this goes sideways, I've got nothing. I need him to drink that water.

CHAPTER 33:
ACTION IN THE CHURCH

Saturday, 14 February 2015, 1935 hours
Shawn's headquarters, Huancayo, Peru

"Here you go, Shawn," Eddy offered. "Take a long drink. You look a little flushed."

Actually, you do.

Shawn was in a good mood now that the obstacles to his money had been removed. He took the water bottle from Eddy and unscrewed the cap. He was about to take a long drink when Frederico approached him, dragging a body.

Frederico narrowed his eyes and looked in Eddy's direction. "I went up on the tower for my normal checks, saw goofball there talking to this guy. Next thing I know; Manuel is being carried away. This useless bag of bones knocked Manuel out. I would've taken this guy out along with the traitor you're talking to, but there were too many witnesses in the street. I called you on the radio, Shawn, but I didn't get an answer. I figure Eddy here has some other friends lurking out there. We can get it out of him."

Pete? Eddy could only see the cargo pants. It was Pete. Did this guy kill him?

Eddy trembled and found that he couldn't speak. His vision started to fade, and he felt weak, just like when he had his blood drawn.

I'm going into shock!

He inhaled and exhaled slowly, just like the Army doctor had taught him to do.

Shawn glared at Eddy. He had to know pushing Eddy would only result in Eddy passing out, and that wouldn't answer any questions. So, Shawn and Fred stood there scowling while Eddy calmed down.

Although Eddy was no longer in danger of passing out, he was still filled with adrenaline.

Shawn's nose was curled up, with his nostrils pointing to the left side of his face, the way they always did when he was irritated. "What the fuck is going on, Eddy? What did you do to Manuel?"

Excuses ran through Eddy's head. He was nauseous when he saw the blood near Pete's body. It was beginning to form a puddle. Eddy saw where Pete had apparently been stabbed.

OK, Eddy, you need to stall for a little bit. They haven't found Wise Dog yet.

Eddy said, "Sounds like Fred here has been sampling some of the medicinal weed. Let's go look at the key and make sure it works so we can get you your money, Shawn. Then, I need my pay. After that, we can talk about whatever it is Fred thinks he saw."

Frederico shouted, "What are you saying? I made this up? Killed someone for nothing? Pulled the key myself? Where is Manuel? You think I'm some idiot?"

Eddy remarked, "I would never use the word smart in the same sentence with your name, Fred."

Frederico made a move to teach him a lesson, but Eddy had worked his way down to his right cargo pocket to retrieve the Browning Hi-Power, which was made of steel, unlike the polymer Glock. Eddy pulled it out by the barrel and used it as a blunt instrument, pistol-whipping Frederico as he grabbed the Sig Sauer pistol on his right hip.

True to form, Shawn made a quick exit.

I'm shocked, Eddy thought sarcastically.

Eddy charged his weapon. Frederico dove behind a pew, grabbing for the Sig. Eddy shot him in the right shoulder—not fatal, but it dropped him. The pistol clattered to the floor. Frederico clutched his wound, trying to slow the bleeding.

Wise Dog ran from the other end of the church, holding a revolver in front of him. He seemed stunned for a moment when his eyes landed on Pete's still form, but then his training kicked in and Wise Dog checked for a pulse.

"He's dead."

"Who do we need to kill?" Wise Dog asked.

Eddy looked at Pete again but didn't speak. After a pause, he said, "Where's Shawn?"

"I don't know. I was fighting the Latin Lover here, and Shawn ran off."

Wise Dog dropped to one knee, yanking Frederico's arms behind him. The rasp of plastic ties cut through Frederico's ragged groans as wrists and ankles snapped tight. From a pouch, Wise Dog pulled a bandage, pressing it hard against the wound until Frederico hissed. "You stay here with stupid. I'm going after our target. The back entrance is locked. If he runs by here, you'll see him." He picked up the Sig Sauer, checked that it was loaded and set to fire, then drew a small flashlight. Holding it steady over his left wrist, he moved out.

Eddy turned on the laser sight on his Browning, then pulled the Glock 43 from his crotch and tucked it into the back of his waistband, just like Wise Dog had done. He held the Browning in a Weaver stance[6], both hands locked in.

He heard Wise Dog moving from room to room, clearing each one. Occasionally, Eddy spotted him through gaps in the pews, but mostly, he was out of view.

---

6   **Weaver Stance**: A classic two-handed pistol shooting position developed by Jack Weaver in the 1950s. The shooter stands with the support-side foot forward, strong-side foot back, and knees slightly bent. The shooting arm extends forward with a slight bend, while the support arm bends more sharply, pulling back to create isometric tension. This push-pull dynamic stabilizes the weapon and helps control recoil. The torso leans slightly forward, and the grip is firm with both hands. Though once widely used, many modern shooters now favor the isosceles stance for quicker target transitions and better compatibility with contemporary optics.

The door to the second floor creaked open. Footsteps echoed as Wise Dog climbed the stone stairs, the wooden banisters groaning under the weight. He swept the upper level, methodical and fast, just like the floor below. As he passed the bathroom, he didn't hesitate. A hesitation would have gotten him killed.

He stepped past a thin wooden door. A shotgun blast blew splinters into his side.

The blast boomed through the building. Eddy ducked behind a pew, yanked the Glock from his waistband, and braced for a fight.

Wise Dog staggered, lost his balance, and crashed into a chair in the dark hallway. His ankle twisted on the way down.

Shawn sprinted for the stairs with the shotgun. He was desperate now. Dangerous.

There was one room Wise Dog hadn't cleared. It had a thick metal door. He had skipped it, thinking, *Do the easy ones first.*

That door now opened.

Sam shuffled into the light, clearly high.

"Dude, can a guy get some sleep around here or what?" he yawned.

Shawn shoved him aside, snarling something about him being an idiot, and kept running.

Wise Dog, still on the floor, got on his knees and commanded, "Stop! Don't move!" Wise Dog shouted.

Shawn stopped, backed up, and shoved the shotgun barrel into Sam's side. "Come with me!"

Shawn walked backwards, shielding himself with Sam. They made their way down the stairs.

Changing his mind, Shawn turned Sam and shoved him. "You know what? You go down first."

Sam stumbled and fell to the ground. Shawn grabbed him violently with his hand and forced him back on his feet.

Eddy had gagged and grabbed Fred's phone and put it on speaker. He was trying to reach Donald Delcey, but no answer. Footsteps came down the stairwell.

Sam emerged first. Then Shawn.

Shawn held Sam like a shield again. He shut and locked the door behind him.

Moves fast, Eddy had to admit.

Time to take control.

"OK, Shawn, let Sam go, and you can walk out of here for now. I can't compete with a shotgun, but I bet I can hit you once, and you are very delicate."

Eddy watched as Shawn seemed to weigh his options. He could have pushed Sam forward, knowing Eddy wouldn't risk hurting him, and run for the door. At this point, Eddy could see that Shawn was armed not only with the shotgun but also with what looked like a Glock 22 on his hip.

Shawn said, "How about this: you set your pistol down, and I don't paint the wall with Sam."

Wise Dog struggled down the stairs.

"No, that isn't going to work. You never give up your gun." He is never going to shoot someone when they work as a shield/leverage for him.

Shawn moved slowly toward the front of the church, keeping Sam between himself and Eddy. Sam was only halfway aware of what was happening. Eddy could hear Wise Dog pounding on the stairwell door, trying to force it open.

The front door creaked open.

Father Benavides stepped inside, calm and silent.

Shawn turned, just a glance, but it was all the priest needed. He stepped forward and drove both hands into Shawn's back, shoving him straight toward Eddy and knocking down Sam. Sam crawled off to Eddy's left and whimpered in a corner clearly in shock. *My God, I need a joint.*

Eddy stepped in and drove an uppercut under Shawn's chin, quick, clean, and just like Wise Dog taught him. Bone cracked, and Shawn dropped.

Father Benavides looked at Eddy, eyes steady. "Wise Dog came to see me," he said. "Said he needed a confession."

Sam collapsed, then crawled into a corner and broke down in tears.

Wise Dog limped in, the Sig lowered, but ready. "You just had to beat me to it, didn't you?" he said.

"I didn't mean to," Eddy muttered.

Wise Dog turned to Father Benavides. "What the hell are you doing here?"

Father Benavides looked at Wise Dog. "Talking to you gave me the courage to confront him. I came to reason with him again. Even if he threatened my family, I couldn't keep pretending he hadn't poisoned this town."

Wise Dog pulled out his phone and called Marcus Snooten at Silent Wolf. Pete was dead, and that needed some explaining. The mission may not have been official, but losing one of their own still demanded a report.

Wise Dog checked his watch. The whole fight had taken only twenty minutes.

"Where the hell do we even start?" Eddy muttered, eyes scanning the wreckage. "This thing went sideways fast."

Wise Dog handled the cleanup soon afterwards. He dug steadily, the scrape of the shovel mixing with the rustle of leaves overhead. When the ground was ready, he eased Pete's body down and covered it with soil, patting the mound flat with the back of the shovel.

He stood a moment, head bowed, and whispered a few words before turning back toward the trail.

The Federal Marshals were contacted. After calls to Tommy Chong, then Angie, and finally the Peruvian government, they secured a charter flight to Lima to bring Shawn, Manuel, and Frederico back to face justice.

Under pressure, Shawn gave up the codes to the offshore accounts. The money was wired back to Trufunds. The crypto angle never made the news.

CHAPTER 34: HEADSHOT

Tommy Chong hired Eddy to work corporate security, which he eagerly accepted. These days, Eddy often goes on dive trips to the Caribbean, realizing that *tomorrow is never promised.* He felt good about bringing Shawn to justice. He traded in his Kona Blue 2012 Mustang and bought himself a Jet Black 1967 Mustang Retromod for special occasions. Eddy was often at the gun range in Grapevine.

He drove a Winter Green Mercedes SUV from his house in Grapevine to Trufunds. It was a company car, but it might as well have been his. He didn't have to be there at a specific time, but he needed to put in eight hours today.

Although a flawed man, Carlos Ortiz, the CEO of Trufunds, was not ungrateful. He'd made a lot of money off the funds he gambled with, and the clients never lost a dollar. He'd successfully used their accounts to buy and trade stocks, which was illegal. Scared by his close call, Carlos never gambled again. Instead, he funneled the money he'd gained into charities, always anonymously.

The fallout gave him time to reflect. Apparently, he learned something from it.

As Eddy pulled into the parking lot, a balding man with brown hair stood in front of his reserved space. The guy looked like he'd seen better days. Yet, he wasn't dressed poorly, and he was lean.

The man moved so Eddy could park.

Eddy stepped out, and the man became noticeably nervous. Eddy felt the Glock 19 in the belt holster beneath his suit jacket.

The man took a hesitant step forward and said, "Hi, Eddy. Shawn says he forgives you, and he'll see you soon."

Then he ran off.

Eddy called after him, but the guy kept running.

He took a quick snapshot with his phone.

The encounter shook him. Shawn was on trial for murder. He'd plea-bargained and got his capital charges reduced because he rolled over on his drug network, which the DEA had been pursuing for years.

Inside, Eddy spoke with Mr. Ortiz and a few coworkers. After a few phone calls, he realized Shawn was out on bail. The sentence reduction and sweet-talking lawyer had done the trick. Shawn's clean behavior didn't hurt either.

The following two weeks passed uneventfully.

Eddy was home that Thursday. He was tired and hadn't been sleeping well. Most people wouldn't sleep well after the goon of a murderous narcissist showed up to deliver a message.

ꜱ$$$$ꜱ

Friday, 29 May 2015, 1030 hours

"Come on, baby, it's time for another walk," Eddy called to Dina, his dog.

The warm sun felt good, and dew still clung to the grass. Eddy felt alive and laughed a little. They had a playful tug-of-war with the leash. She was house-trained but full of energy, like most German Shepherds.

They walked around the neighborhood. The only thing that seemed out of place was a black Range Rover SUV with dark windows. Eddy had never seen it before. It moved slowly, as if the driver were searching for something.

After the walk, he let Dina back inside. He'd give her a bath later.

Eddy grabbed a rake and started on the yard.

He saw the Range Rover again. It was settled by a coffee shop, far enough to avoid suspicion but close enough to stir his curiosity.

Oh well, not everything is a mystery.

He kept raking, occasionally glancing toward the SUV. Then a car door slammed behind him.

It was a red Ford F-150 with an extended cab. Two rough-looking men stepped out. Both wore blue jeans with black belts and dark, buttoned shirts. Their hair was too long to be military. They wore sunglasses and looked fit, like lumberjacks. One carried a shotgun. They stood outside of the truck and waited for Shawn.

Yes, it was broad daylight in a middle to upper-middle-class neighborhood, but people in Grapevine worked. They had to, to afford to live there.

Shawn stepped out from the back of the truck. He wore jeans and a brown T-shirt. The three of them approached Eddy, moving slowly, only Shawn smiling, the other two indifferent.

Really out of place, Eddy thought. But now wasn't the time to analyze his wardrobe. Shawn wasn't there to make peace. Eddy knew that before he even stepped out of the truck.

Shawn called out with a wide smile and a voice too loud for the moment. "Don't worry, Eddy, we made sure nobody else was home. Ironic, isn't it? The best time to do this was in broad daylight. Your dog and security system made anything else a bad decision."

That same smug grin Eddy hated.

Eddy processed it fast, eyes hunting for a way out. One look told him the two men with Shawn could break him in a fight.

"It's over, Shawn. You've got a great lawyer. Just go that route," Eddy said, buying time. He knew Shawn had to have the last word.

He felt the Glock under his sweatshirt. They had waited until Dina was inside. She wouldn't even know anything had happened. Keep him talking. He loves his own voice.

"Well, I see you couldn't do it yourself. Got others to do your work, as usual."

Eddy lifted his left hand to scratch his face, hoping to distract them long enough to grab the pistol.

"Shut up. I'm tired of hearing your nonsense. I treated you like a brother. You betrayed me. I helped you out, got you work, saved your life," Shawn said.

"Shawn, again, you didn't save my life in Costa Rica. You're not the savior of the world. You're just some guy who doesn't like to work." Eddy taunted, "Why do you need that goon to kill me? Not man enough to do it yourself?"

Shawn's face turned beet red. "Give me that fucking shotgun!" he barked, ripping it from the nearest thug's hands.

He didn't notice Eddy turning, left side facing him, dropping the rake as a distraction. He released the holster's safety with his thumb.

"I'll finish you myself. I won't have to listen to your mouth anymore," Shawn growled.

Eddy spoke calmly, hand inching toward the pistol. "Well, I went to Afghanistan to win hearts and minds. That didn't pan out. But I'm going straight to your heart and mind." *Well, technically, center of mass, not the heart.*

Eddy smiled.

Shawn pumped the shotgun. "What the hell are you even talking about?"

Eddy drew the Glock 19. No cocking needed. His first two shots struck Shawn's chest in center mass, near the heart, and the third hit just above his eyes.

Two in the heart and one in the mind, thought Eddy. He thanked Winston for his close-quarters training.

Shawn Michael Larson, con artist, liar, cheat, murderer, womanizer, and fraud, collapsed into a spreading pool of blood. The final round had taken off part of his skull and scattered fragments across the lawn.

He stood over Shawn's body with no satisfaction. Only closure.

The other two men had pistols, but Eddy moved first. He dropped to one knee and aimed. Seven rounds remained.

"Don't move. Try it, and I'll drop you."

He grabbed his cell and dialed 911 with his left hand.

I'll shoot before you draw. Take your pistols out, fingers off the trigger, and drop them. Kick them over here. One false move and I'll shoot."

Kicking them close wasn't likely, but he had no time to think of anything better.

One man did as he was told.

The other man hesitated.

"Drop it!" Eddy shouted.

The man dropped it, then reached for a second weapon in the small of his back.

Eddy spotted the glint of a stainless-steel barrel and fired one round.

The shot hit the man's left leg. He screamed, cursing, and rolled in pain. A stainless steel .38 revolver lay on the grass.

Eddy pointed at the remaining man. "Just stay where you are. I don't know if you're Beavis or Butthead[7], but hit the ground. Chest down. Arms forward."

Eddy resumed his weaver stance with feet staggered, pistol firm in both hands, elbows locked.

---

7   **Beavis and Butthead** was a cartoon showing two teenage boys behaving in socially unacceptable ways.

EPILOGUE

Friday, 29 May 2015, 1800 hours
Eddy's home, Grapevine, Texas

Eddy's phone rang, and he answered it before the second ring, thinking it was the police.

"Hello?"

"Mr. Ludt, so pleased to finally make your acquaintance. Please call me Javier," a man with a strong accent that Eddy guessed was Spanish said.

"I'm sorry, I don't know who you are," Eddy replied.

"No, you do not. And whether you ever do is completely up to you. The man you killed, who you knew as Shawn, used to work for us. He was highly trained, as you no doubt noticed. Our training is not in traditional fighting but in the more subtle arts of espionage," Javier explained.

"Who is this?" Eddy asked, thinking it was some sick joke.

It seemed that Javier anticipated the question. "Let me assure you, Eddy, this is no joke. I watched the whole incident with Shawn take place. I had nothing to do with what occurred. We were following Shawn, and not you. These men did not carry out my wishes, and I was not entirely sure what their intentions were, but I

217

knew they meant to harm you. It is somewhat barbaric, I admit, but it served as a test for my organization."

There was a brief pause before Javier continued, "You passed, by the way, or you would not be alive. We do the things that must be done, the things that nobody wants to talk about so that others can live their lives in peace under the illusion of a civilized society. Many governments know about us, and some even fear us, but none acknowledge us. What I can assure you, Eddy, is that we strive for the greater good and are funded by those organizations that recognize our true intentions while simultaneously denying our existence."

Eddy could feel the hair rising on his neck.

"OK, and why should I believe a word you say?" He felt a little scared.

"Eddy, don't be so nervous. We are the good guys, and the choice must be yours. You will never be able to expose us. I can assure you of that. You will not even find a record of this call. I appreciate you taking care of Shawn. He was efficient but evil. We knew he had flaws when we recruited him, but we didn't realize how severe they were.

How did he know that?

"If you are interested, call this number back. Do not text. This number will only work once. Leave a message on the recorder. I'm sorry we could not intervene on your behalf. We had to know that you were ready and that you had it in you to fight and even kill when necessary.

"The when necessary is important. Shawn grew to love it, and when that happens, you are lost. You can stop working if you want to, and you can pursue that doctorate that you always wanted."

There was silence, and then Eddy heard a dial tone.

Wait, how did he know I wanted a doctorate?

Saturday, 30 May 2015, 1821 hours
Don Delcey's home, Tampa, Florida

Don and Eddy sat on Don's front porch, drinking Heinekens and smoking Cuban cigars.

"I don't understand. Where did this guy come from? We still don't know what he did or who he was for the first twenty-one years of his life," Don asked.

Eddy kept quiet. He hadn't told anyone about Javier. It all seemed so strange to him. He had done his job well. It was either Shawn or him, and Eddy had done what he had to do to survive. He was happy at his home in Grapevine with his dog.

"We need some more brewskies. I'll walk down to the gas station and get us some more beer."

Eddy countered, "That's OK, I got it. I need to lose some more weight, anyway. The walk will do me good."

He walked down the road. It was a mixture of rundown and new houses, as well as numerous high-end apartment complexes. The presence of the military and other factors changed the dynamics of this town. The residents were a mix, too. Families who'd arrived years ago when it was less expensive and those who hadn't lived there as long, both renters and buyers.

Eddy crossed the street cautiously, as many people who came down from the Northeast didn't seem to notice pedestrians. It wasn't that they were necessarily bad drivers or under the influence; they simply felt entitled to do as they pleased.

There were no sidewalks on this street, so Eddy hurried along the grass. Broken beer bottles lay in his path, so he paid extra attention.

Eddy saw the sign for "Freddy's Gas and Grub". There were four gas pumps, two of them occupied. At one sat a recent model orange Corvette, and at the other was a black Range Rover SUV, whose occupants remained inside.

He entered the building and noticed through the window a large, very tall, and muscular man step out of the driver's side of the SUV.

Eddy went inside to use the restroom, no doubt the effect of the two beers, which he'd consumed in about fifteen minutes.

After exiting the restroom, Eddy grabbed a six-pack of Heineken from the cooler and approached the cashier to pay with his credit card.

"Good evening," Eddy said. The cashier had a pale complexion, long brown hair, glasses, and an intelligent look about her. She wore faded jeans and a white T-shirt with a picture of a rock band on it and had a series of tattoos going up and down her arms.

"Some Mr. Universe-looking guy was just in here and said to give this to you. A reminder from Javier." She pulled a small black plastic bag from beneath the counter as she spoke. Astonished, Eddy immediately looked around for the SUV but saw that it had already left. "Can you give me a little more of a description of that man, please? I just want to make sure who it is."

She described him as best she could, and Eddy made notes on his phone. He walked outside, sat on the bench, and carefully opened the sealed plastic bag. Inside, he found a white box with a personalized card that read:

Eddy, I realize you might think my call was a prank or that you're being pulled into something shady. Honestly, if I were in your position, I'd probably think the same. So, I don't blame you for being hesitant. To obtain fidelity in this matter, a man of your intelligence would need further evidence. I have included information about you that a prank caller would never know. Rest assured that this information will never be shared, either by me or by anyone in my organization, with anyone. Things that Shawn, as you knew him, didn't know about you. Things that most of your best friends never knew. Please consider joining our organization. We need people who lack your familial ties and have your unique skills. I would be happy to give you proof that you are one of the good guys, and you will be rewarded handsomely for your endeavors.

Inside the box was a small black notebook. In it were typed many personal things about Eddy that demonstrated just how much Javier knew. Things Eddy hadn't shared with anyone.

On the cover page was written: The biggest fan of your work, Javier.

The notebook was so small that it fit in his jeans pocket. He decided to go easy on the beer to keep a clear head.

Eddy slowly returned to Don's small but comfortable house, with only two cars passing him on the way back.

Don asked, "What were you doing, making the beer from scratch? You were gone for over an hour. I was ready to send out a rescue party. You need a personal locator beacon, bro."

Eddy wasn't really paying attention, and his eyes wandered as he spoke. "No, I'm sorry, man. I got caught up talking to someone."

Javier wanted me to know that he was for real, but I don't think that he is a threat.

Previously, he'd worked because he had to. Now Eddy had a job he liked and enough money. Who knows what he would ask me to do? I know what I want to do, and I'm going to do it now.

Javier was interested enough in him to track him down and wait for just the right moment to have someone give Eddy the bag with the notebook. Eddy was intrigued. *Was it a trick?*

Well, for now, I'll continue in my job with the bank for a few more years and then become a full-time student studying Spanish, earn my PhD, and write books, specifically crime or spy thrillers.

If anyone was silly enough to pay me to do it, all the better. Maybe I could even write a book about my life. No, nobody would pay to read a book about my life. It isn't exciting enough.

Eddy admitted to people now that he'd made that head shot on Ghost One by accident. A complete screwup, really. But nobody seemed to believe him. His escapades in Peru were never publicized, but people talked. He knew now that survival wasn't about strength or even about luck. It was about seeing the world for what it was, broken, brutal, but still somehow beautiful. He hadn't changed because he wanted to. He'd changed because he had to. And somehow, that was enough.

Rumors swirled in the Special Forces community. They spoke of an intel guy. Just a geek, really. But the story went that he had turned out to be a crack shot. The same guy who took out mercenaries in the jungle and dragged a wanted man back to the U.S., then gunned him down, gunslinger style.

Most of it sounded like a legend. That's how these stories always are.

But Eddy's mind stayed on Javier. Elusive. Enigmatic. Oddly convincing. And tied to something far bigger than Eddy had ever imagined.

He hated to admit it.

But he wanted to know more.

Thank you for choosing my book among so many others. I hope you enjoyed the journey! If you did, I'd love to hear your thoughts, did it resonate with you, would you recommend it to others?

Your review on Amazon or Goodreads not only helps me grow as a writer but also helps other readers discover the book.

GLOSSARY OF TERMS

Beavis and Butthead: A cartoon showing two teenage boys behaving in socially unacceptable ways.

Chicha de jora: A drink, either fermented or not, made from maize—yellow, white, or purple corn, depending on the region.

FISH: Forensic Information System for Handwriting.

Go bag: Military slang for a bag prepared in case a military member needs to leave in a hurry due to an emergency of some sort.

Going loud: is slang used in the U.S. military to mean: "no more need for stealth." Use weapons freely, noise and light discipline is less important than lethality.

GOMOR: General Officer Memorandum of Reprimand. A formal written reprimand issued by a General Officer (typically a one-star or above). It can be: Administrative (filed locally): Only seen by the command—doesn't follow the soldier. Permanent, goes in the Army Military Human Resource Record, and can end a career.

Groups: U.S. Army Special Forces units are divided into Groups. The 7th Special Forces Group operates in South America, and the 10th Special Forces Group operates in

Europe. Other Special Forces Groups operate in different geographical locations.

VFW: Stands for Veterans of Foreign Wars. In this instance, the reference is to a VFW bar, where service members who served in the U.S. military during a time of combat operations and their families can enjoy discounted liquor and select food items.

Weaver Stance: A classic two-handed pistol shooting position developed by Jack Weaver in the 1950s. The shooter stands with the support-side foot forward, strong-side foot back, and knees slightly bent. The shooting arm extends forward with a slight bend, while the support arm bends more sharply, pulling back to create isometric tension. This push-pull dynamic stabilizes the weapon and helps control recoil. The torso leans slightly forward, and the grip is firm with both hands. Though once widely used, many modern shooters now favor the isosceles stance for quicker target transitions and better compatibility with contemporary optics.

ABOUT THE AUTHOR

Kenneth Edward Webb was born in Collingdale, Pennsylvania, just outside of Philadelphia. He spent his early years in Pennsylvania and New Jersey before moving to Texas, where he graduated from high school in Colleyville. He earned a bachelor's degree in English from the University of Texas at Arlington and, nearly two decades later, returned to school to complete a Master of Arts in Intelligence Studies at American Military University.

Ken is a retired U.S. Army Reserve officer, having served for 33 years serving in both military police and military intelligence. Nearly 18 of those years were spent on active duty. He is also retired from American Airlines.

He now lives in Miraflores, Peru, where he wrote this novel, studies Spanish at *El Sol* language school, and is preparing to pursue his doctorate. He considers himself a lifelong learner—someone who finds meaning in growth, discipline, and the pursuit of knowledge. His passions include scuba diving, hiking, reading, writing, travel, and the quiet strategy of a good game of chess.

Trapped in Deception is his first novel. Writing it has been a therapeutic journey—one that helped him make sense of complex experiences while crafting a story that he hopes will keep readers fully engaged. In developing the book, Ken conducted extensive research to strengthen the plot and characters. More than anything, he wanted this debut to be a story that not only holds the reader's attention but also earns their time.

Readers are invited to connect with Ken Webb on their preferred social network. Simply scan the QR code or enter the provided URL in your browser.

https://bit.ly/m/kenwebb

ACKNOWLEDGEMENTS

Bringing this book to life has been a journey marked by growth, grit, and grace. I could not have done it alone.

To my **Alpha and Beta Readers**—thank you for walking alongside me from the rough beginnings to the final polish. A special thanks to **Barry Campbell**, who read through many iterations and offered honest, constructive feedback that sharpened the narrative. I am especially grateful to **Leila Majaj Kirkconnell**, whose contributions went far beyond expectations. Her meticulous Beta reading, formatting of the table of contents, and overall refinement of the manuscript were invaluable.

To the many fellow writers and creatives who encouraged me to keep going when the path seemed long—you know who you are—thank you for believing in this story and in me.

This book is more than a story—it's a bucket list item and a personal work of art. It was not written for profit but created from a desire to craft something meaningful. My hope is that it offers something beautiful for others to experience, reflect on, and enjoy.

Everyone in this book is based on someone I know. And outside of the illegal activities, most of these events really happened. The truth, as they say, is often stranger—and more compelling—than fiction.

This book carries my name, but it was built on the support, insight, and encouragement of others. I am deeply grateful.